The Misplaced

Ghost Hunting With Chris Abeyta

An Angel Falls Novella

Jody A. Kessler

Please visit:
www.JodyAKessler.com
Sign up for the newsletter

ISBN: 978-1546928973
E book ASIN: B0719GKZ4X

Edited by
Melissa A. Robitille

Cover Art & Design by
Laura Moyer

Manufactured in the United States of America
First Edition

Other Works Available

An Angel Falls series

Death Lies Between Us #1
Angel Dreams #2
Haunting Me #3
Book #4 coming soon
The Misplaced – An Angel Falls Novella with Chris Abeyta
The Call – An Angel Falls Novella with Chris Abeyta

Historical Time Travel series
The Night Medicine

Witches of Lane County
Heart of the Secret #1
A Witch's Fate #2

Granite Lake Romance
Unwrapping Treasure #1
Chasing Treasure #2

&

A New Adult Coming of Age Novel

When We're Entwined

Dedication

To the seekers, dreamers, and misfits.

Chapter One

"RISE AND SHINE, porcupine."

Chris cracked open sleep encrusted eyes. "Can I help you?" His throat rasped, and his body groaned, begging to return to sleep.

"I don't know, but I definitely want to find out."

The amount of perkiness in her voice made Chris cringe and wish he slept with earplugs.

"Come again?" He glanced at the clock on his dresser. Four-fourteen a.m. As an early riser, this should not have been quite such a shock to his system. But he went to bed late after a grueling night of spiritual cleansing, and an unexpected battle with a particularly spiteful ghost, at the local pool hall. Professional ghost hunter and shaman, Chris Abeyta, was dog-tired, bushed, and mentally unprepared for… anything that didn't involve staring at the back of his eyelids.

Rolling over, he ignored his visitor. His exhausted mind and body deserved one full night's rest. More like a year's worth of sleep. He'd settle for eight hours. The soul residing within him, however, could not ignore the woman standing over the bed. A feminine and luminous quality, added to captivating eyes, taunted his sleep-addled brain. Perhaps he only imagined the halo of light surrounding her abundant hair. What color is her hair?

Black? No, not black, burgundy? No, not that either. Darker than auburn, but not black. *Damn. Thinking clearly on two hours of sleep is not happening.*

"Yoo-hoo," she sang.

The attention getter registered but didn't make him turn over and face her.

"Not yet." Chris didn't know if the grumble was spoken aloud or not. He didn't care. He needed to decipher the exact color of her hair. Why her eyes looked so painfully familiar. In his current state of bone-deep exhaustion these details seemed absolutely vital before abandoning the comfort of his mattress. Chestnut? Sable? A cross between the two. That's it. Blackened chestnut. There. He'd done it. Solved yet another mystery. Now, about those eyes. Brown? He thought so. He'd been so fixed on the waves of shiny blackened chestnut that her eye color didn't stick. It might be the distraction of her eyebrows. Sculpted, sleek, and expressive. Yes, the eyebrows perfectly complimented the hair. Lips, nose, cheekbones. They accentuated each other on a sensual and attractive oval face. He hadn't thought any female remarkably beautiful since meeting Juliana Crowson. Sure, he appreciated a feminine figure and a nice smile here or there, but no one ever stood out enough to garner a second look.

Chris liked bachelorhood. Not only liked it but preferred it. He and women were at odds. No. That wasn't totally accurate. He and people, in general, were at odds. It was a choice he made daily, but in actuality more a genetic default or birth inheritance. When Chris Abeyta entered this world, Great Spirit took one look at him and declared, "This one. The chubby-cheeked vibrant son of

Sherman White Wolf Abeyta will be gifted many powerful medicines to be used for healing. He will have clear vision and insights into the ghost worlds. He will use his gifts to help those who suffer, and assist others who need help finding the Good Red Road."

Nowhere did Great Spirit mention people skills or a getting along with the human race. It showed. Chris could hardly stand being with himself, let alone anyone else. Particularly those who made life more challenging. So, pretty much everyone, in every conceivable way. He grew up as a solitary participant. He learned to become a shaman from his father and made a few friends along the way. A father and friends he rarely ever saw. Keeping his distance benefitted everyone, especially him. He tolerated his clients only long enough to aid their spiritual needs. He would deal with a haunting, perform a ceremony, or do whatever else they needed from him. Most of the time, Chris just wanted to be left alone.

Juliana was the only friend he made since returning home from University — almost four years ago. If he could call her a friend. One friend every four years. The thought plagued him. Sixteen years from now, a handful of people would bother him on a regular basis. It's time to cut someone loose, he thought.

It would not be Juliana. His apprentice needed more training. Somehow, Juliana Crowson managed to wedge herself into his life and obliterate his better judgment. She had intrigued him at first. Not just because of her looks and her half-Native bloodline, but also her natural abilities to see and hear the afterlife and its occupants. She had absolutely no inkling of what to do with her gifts. The danger she put herself in astounded Chris. He couldn't stand by and let her be killed. She surely would have been if he hadn't intervened. His lessons with Juliana on the afterlife progressed slowly, but steadily, and he was satisfied with her development. Last night, she proved again her willingness to be scared witless, yet do as instructed, to bring balance and harmony to the spirit world.

"Listen up, Sleeping Beauty. I understand the need to sleep it off. Believe me, I do. I've been hung-over a time or two myself, but there's no time for a morning cuddle and a long chat over coffee. Get up right now or I'm going to make you!"

He shoved all thoughts concerning Juliana aside. The mystery woman demanding his attention rose to the forefront. Chris groaned again, and the reverberation traveled through his body all the way down to his toes.

Last night should have gone a whole lot smoother. When he'd been in the attic above the pool hall, the spirit he'd been chasing led him straight to a section amidst the rafters that had no floorboards. Chris hadn't seen it. He was too busy casting the varmint into the hereafter to pay attention to the missing floor. Falling and banging his shin on a joist had been unfortunate. Hitting his head on the rafters had just been humiliating, and painful. The impish ghost thought it rather hilarious.

The case had been interesting. Chris wanted to take the time to ponder over the unusual details of what transpired last night. In the past, the billiard hall and bar had never seen any spiritual or otherworldly trouble. Chris wanted to know what had changed. It could be as simple as a patron bringing a nasty spirit with them into the building, but Chris's instincts told him otherwise.

Something seemed out of sorts. He needed to figure it out. Otherwise, the owners of the building might be calling him back. Not that he failed to send the mischievous spirit to the afterlife. He succeeded, and Juliana gained valuable hands-on experience. When he finally left sometime after midnight, he didn't have the sense of closure that normally went with a completed job.

All that would need to wait. Sleeping off the headache was his first priority. That, too, should fall to the wayside, as far as his unexpected visitor was concerned. Four more hours of rest would make life bearable. Was it really too much to ask? Didn't this woman come with a built-in snooze button? How about a mute switch?

Chris smelled cigarette smoke and determined he had to be dreaming. She wouldn't light up inside his cabin, would she? That level of disrespect and bad manners? Unthinkable, and unheard of in his personal space. It was a dream. A dream where he remembered the smell of the smoking lounge at the back of the pool hall last night.

"Beep…beep…beep…beep!"

Chris launched himself out of bed and saw his uninvited guest standing on the corner of his mattress holding a lit cigarette up to the smoke detector. The piercing wail penetrated every cell in his fatigued body and made his ears cry for relief. She brought the cigarette to her lips, inhaled, and blew a long stream of smoke toward the ceiling.

"Told you I'd make you get up." She jumped down from the bed before Chris could snatch the cigarette from her impudent fingers. The cigarette had the distinct spicy scent of clove mixed with tobacco. No matter. He still didn't like it or want it in his house.

Mystery woman scooted out of the room, and he didn't pursue her. Instead, he reached up and jammed the tip of his finger against the minuscule button to shut off the alarm.

With a sigh that didn't relieve his exasperation, exhaustion, or impatience, he glanced out the bedroom window and saw nothing but the blessed dark. The dark he longed to return to in the form of sleep.

"We're running out of time, sleepy head," she called from the direction of his living room.

"Time for what?" he said with no enthusiasm and the barest minimum of curiosity.

"Oh, you know, the usual. Saving souls and protecting the planet."

Chris didn't bother looking for her before changing into a pair of cargo pants and a fresh shirt. He shuffled down the hall wondering if she continued to pollute his cabin with her cigarette. He no longer smelled it, but more importantly, he wanted to know why she showed up there at all. The woman, with the wildly curly multi-colored hair, was not in his living room when he entered.

"You may need your medicine bag," she said from behind him.

Chris spun one-eighty and headed to the back of the cabin to his sunroom and workroom.

"Explain yourself."

His unnamed guest perused the workbench and had her nose stuck in the top of a jar of copal.

"I always enjoyed burning copal. It's a necessity for someone like myself."

"Who are you?" Chris asked.

"A girl who needs your help. We really don't have time for jibber-jabber. Grab your tools and let's get out of here."

"Refusing to answer will only force me to make you leave. Your behavior is unacceptable."

She set the jar down and turned a beguiling gaze on him. Chris refused to be bewitched by this stunning woman in his sunroom. Her face might be appealing and her body attractive, nearly every curve highlighted in her tight stretch pants and a long sweater, but it would take a lot more than physical beauty to persuade him to blindly follow. So far, she had not provided any reason to go with her.

"You need to take me back to the pool hall. Now. Before someone gets hurt."

"Did you follow me home?"

"No. I mean yes, and no. I don't know."

Confusion tangled with apprehension on her face. Chris didn't like seeing either emotion. "What is your name?"

"Naomi Hutson."

He knew she wasn't lying. Chris always knew when someone lied to him. Auras gave them away, and if there were no aura because they belonged to the ethereal realm, he still read their eyes and their body language. Even if her answers were obscure, she was honest about her name.

"I did not see you at Jack's Corner Pocket." The pool hall and smoking club had been busy, but Chris would have noticed her. He considered it part of his job as a ghost hunter and shaman to pay attention to everything in his domain when working a case. Not to mention, this woman stood out. She would ping on his radar immediately.

She shrugged as if to say, not her problem, but the solemn pleading in her eyes couldn't be ignored.

"The entire town is in danger, Mr. Abeyta. I'm in grave danger. We need your help, and we need it now."

Chapter Two

URGENCY PROPELLED Chris from where he stood rooted to the plank flooring of his workroom to the front of his cabin. He perched on the edge of his recliner and shoved his feet inside the boots he only unlaced a few hours earlier. Naomi stood like a sentinel near the front door waiting for him. Chris stumbled outside, sleep deprived and dragging. They climbed into his Toyota pickup truck and drove into town.

"This is better, isn't it? We're on the move. Just a pagan girl and a cranky shaman off to save the day."

From the sound of it, her mood had lightened ten thousand percent. She forgot her somber doom and gloom. Chris glanced sideways and contemplated kicking her out of the cab. At this time of day, severe and apocalyptic was much easier to handle than cheerful. He had not forgotten or dismissed her comments inside the cabin. Combined with what she'd said, she leaned heavily toward a chipper and perky personality. This would not do. *Couldn't he return to the billiard hall alone? It would make things so much easier.*

"Don't even think about it," she said with no prompting.

So, he wasn't the only one inside the truck with the uncanny ability to know what someone was thinking.

"You are leaving out important details about why you're dragging me away from my house in the pre-dawn hours."

"I'd tell you if I knew. Just keep driving. I have a gut feeling we'll both know the details shortly."

"Know what?"

"That's just it. I don't always know what's going to happen. Just that something is going to happen."

"You're an empath without clairvoyance," he said in an attempt to understand who she was.

"I guess you could call it that. I always thought of myself as a witch with a curious amount of off-the-wall skills."

"Witch? As in Wicca or Halloween?"

"Neither. Now stop asking about me. We have to save them. It's up ahead."

"Jack's Corner Pocket is still a few miles from here."

"It is?" Her confused expression was back.

"Yes," Chris said. His inner guidance also sensed an interruption in the awakening of the new day.

Vigilant, spiritually open, and searching, he slowed the truck.

"There!" she said pointing.

Chris sensed the ethereal distortion the same time she did. The pickup veered, and he parked curbside.

"What is it?" she asked.

Chris refrained from answering, grabbed the door handle, and pushed it open. The reek of rotten eggs from sulfur mingled with other minerals assaulted his nose as he stared into a darkened vacant lot next to some retail shops. He ventured toward the empty lot, squinting into the dark and reassessed his previous observation of the brick building next door. One streetlight glowed at the corner of the intersection, and shops waited, boarded up for demolition. Chris tried to remember the last time he visited this part of town and couldn't recall when it was.

"Look at that!" Naomi stabbed a finger toward the back of the empty lot.

She strolled across the construction site to the spot that first captured their attention. Chris followed, taking a little more care to stay alert and aware of their surroundings. He glanced up and down the street, but no one was around at this time of day. Naomi took the lead. Chris followed with little thought regarding the obstructing security fence. *Not much security to it,* he thought as he slipped under the chain holding the gate closed. A small excavator sat parked next to a skid steer, their steel buckets encrusted with dried mud. The fence he promptly ignored was there to protect the expensive machinery more than the torn up ground below his boots. He would make a quick otherworldly assessment and leave.

The lot bordered a tributary of the San Juan River. As he neared the rear of the property, creek water rushed at the bottom of the rocky embankment. Side by side, Chris and Naomi observed the construction site and the beginnings of what looked like a new foundation. Ditches crisscrossed the lot for the infrastructure — whether that was underground sewage lines or gas, Chris didn't know. As they stood there, he understood why Great Spirit had compelled him to pull over and park the truck.

Chris and Naomi stared at the gaping hole in the ground for countless silent seconds. Each caught up in their own thoughts about what lay in front of them. Near the bottom of one trench, a thin spray of water shot six feet into the air from what looked like a broken pipe. The torrent of Earth energy pouring out of the trench couldn't be ignored. It engulfed them in a cloud of steam so dense with ethereal energy the air seemed to vibrate and hum. The pungent smell of the mineral spring water clung to the tiny droplets hanging in the atmosphere around them.

"Looks like someone hit a branch of the geothermal hot springs."

"Mmm-hmm." Chris made a non-specific sound rather than answering.

The area in Southwest Colorado where he lived was well known for its natural hot springs and geothermal activity. Most of the town's businesses used this resource as a natural way to heat the buildings in winter. Swimming and soaking in the local pools were favorite pastimes for the residents of the mountain community, and for thousands of visitors each year. People traveled to his town from all over the world to experience the mineral-rich healing waters.

For Chris, the mineral springs were sacred. Their therapeutic and medicinal benefits could not be compared to any other healing method. When he used the spring water in a healing ceremony, he chose with immense care the source of the spring water. The underground network of rivers and streams was complex, and he had meditated on it many times. Each source where the hot watered surfaced yielded different qualities in the water. The medicine man inside him understood the individual springs had a specific purpose and use. Chris respected the healing water and the unique geothermal activity in the area, and he also understood how much things could change with the development of the town. He glared at the new leak as the sacred water cut a path through the freshly excavated dirt to join the tributary stream a few meters away. Brooding over this find was inevitable, but Chris could not tamp down the thrill of discovery.

"This is why I'm here!" Naomi gushed. She twirled in the mist like a child playing in a sprinkler.

"Here specifically in this town, or more of an existential 'here'?" Chris asked.

She laughed. The sound of it danced through the morning air like small birds singing to the rising sun. "This town! I traveled across the country looking for vortices, and this is the mother vortex! Do you feel it? The surge of energy is incredible. The Earth is alive and amazing!"

Chris definitely felt the vortex, but he wasn't as thrilled with the place of power as she was. Yes, it surged through him and around him. The vibrations in his body rose exponentially from standing so close to it.

"You should dance with me. Dancing brings up your energy level. I think I'll be flying in another few seconds. I can't believe I finally found a natural point of power — like really found it. Not above, or near it, but right freaking here! The water magnifies the energy, doesn't it?"

Chris continued to inspect the ground and the broken pipe. The sky began to lighten in the east, but where they stood remained dark beneath the shadow of the building next door, and the cottonwood trees lining the narrow creek. He held up an LED flashlight on his keychain and shined it into the trench. Whoever dug the ditch had no clue as to what lay beneath. From the sloppy quick-crete surrounding the pipe with a leaking cap, he thought it a botched job all around. Chris pulled his phone out of his vest pocket and took some pictures. The hair rose on his forearms, and he pocketed the phone.

"Someone is coming," he said.

Naomi looked over her shoulder at the street. They saw no approaching vehicles, but Chris heard it or more like felt the vibration through the soles of his boots. A truck, he intuitively knew. Instinct kicked in, and he took a step toward the gate.

"Lay low for a minute," Naomi said. "No one's going to see us way over here."

"I disagree," Chris said. "Let's go now. I've seen enough."

"I'm not done." Instead of following Chris, she edged closer to the trench and tiptoed along the side until she reached the end. Naomi scrambled over a mound of dirt and disappeared.

"Naomi, I am ready to go," Chris tried again.

"I want to see something," she said in the dark.

The fluff of her curls bobbed away as she moved closer to the stream flowing behind the property. If something visceral weren't urging him to get out of sight, he would have followed her. The leaking hot spring ran toward the creek. He wanted to check on the damage from the other side of the ditch and embankment, but not now. Chris assumed Naomi wanted to see the same thing, but he didn't know her and didn't have time to ask. His sixth sense told him the approaching truck was almost there. He skirted across the construction site and ducked behind the excavator just in time to avoid headlights flashing across the lot. Torn between following Naomi and slipping back through the gap in the fence, his hesitation allowed him to watch the work truck pull in front of the gate and stop.

Chris looked back for Naomi but found no sign of her. Just as she said, it was impossible to see where they had been standing. He wished Naomi were next to him so they could go to Jack's Corner Pocket, the location they had originally been headed. *Darn woman. What did she think she was doing?* She insisted on returning to the pool hall at this absurdly early hour and then disappeared.

The door on the pickup truck opened, and a man stepped out. Chris watched from behind the excavator as he unlocked the chain and swung the gate open. The headlights shone his way, and he ducked as the truck drove onto the dirt lot. Listening to the diesel engine rumble while keeping low to the ground, he crept behind the skid steer, prepared to stay in the shadows and slip away unseen. Since foxes are the masters of camouflage, he called the fox's spirit medicine to conceal him from the men in the truck.

The engine quieted, and the doors opened and closed. Two men exited, a driver and one other. Chris paused as a flashlight beam briefly lit the vortex and the ditch. The style of the truck made Chris think they came to repair the broken pipe. Multiple concerns ran through his head. The situation didn't add up. Why work before sunrise? Why did the construction site have an aura about it that figuratively stunk? What part did Naomi play in this? Most importantly, why was Chris guided here to repair what they opened?

Of course, he knew the answer. The energy vortex was too powerful. As soon as he stepped foot on the ground outside his pickup, he felt the overwhelming rush of Earth energy. Vortices were a natural phenomenon that occurred around the globe. The land around Sedona, Arizona being one of the most well-known locations. These natural places of energetic power were also in balance with the Earth. Remaining in harmony with the planet is a key element to survival, at least survival in a healthy manner. The destruction of this lot and rerouting the mineral spring had obvious consequences in Chris's eyes. Although the energy had a positive effect as it erupted from the ground, somewhere else was a polar opposite effect happening to balance this sudden shift.

"She's a traveler. It comes from her father's blood."

Chris slanted his gaze toward Talks to the Wind, his irregular spirit guide. Talks to the Wind came and went on his own schedule. He wasn't overly helpful as spirit guides go. Chris never turned down guidance from his ancestors, but Talks to the Wind's advice rarely pertained to the situation at hand.

"Are you speaking about Naomi?" he whispered.

Talks to the Wind grinned and waggled thin brows. "She is an interesting blend of red, yellow, and dark skinned peoples. It makes for one nice-looking woman. A little narrow in the hips, but she's young. Her hips will widen with age. Then you will have a woman every warrior will want for himself. This is a good, and a bad thing. Maybe you should find an ugly woman that matches your homely face. Then you won't have to worry about losing her to someone better looking than you."

Talks to the Wind needed to stop speaking. This conversation served absolutely no purpose. Not only did Chris have other things on his mind, but discussing Naomi's looks and availability was irrelevant and inappropriate.

Chris narrowed his gaze and wished he'd stop running his mouth or leave. Either option would let Chris concentrate on getting out of there. Now wasn't a good time to catch up with Talks to the Wind or discuss the physical attributes of his... client?

Was Naomi a client? He supposed so. They hadn't officially discussed hiring Chris, but in his line of work, every case was unique. The business end of things was often the last priority. Unsurprisingly, evicting ghosts, calming down poltergeists and assisting lost souls were the main concern. Chris would be paid for his time and expenses in some form or fashion after he took care of the ghost or other disturbance. Enough money found its way into his bank account to keep his bills paid. When a special circumstance called for it, he traded or bartered for services and goods. The cycle of life kept him going, as it had for his father and his father's father.

With hair braided and wearing his buckskins, Talks to the Wind looked like he walked right out of the past. Chris gathered from previous conversations that his guide lived with the Utes long before the European settlers came to this part of America. However, Talks to the Wind had traveled between the spirit world and the physical world for many generations. The Ute brave knew modern customs, spoke English and had an eye for beautiful women — particularly those with dark hair and voluptuous figures.

Since the man would continue to expound on the subject of women if Chris didn't steer the conversation in the direction he wanted, he asked, "What are these men doing here?"

Occasionally, Talks to the Wind would supply something useful to Chris. It didn't happen often, but when it did, Chris would remember why he liked his guide. Since Chris was born, too many spirits to count had assisted him in one way or another. Why or when wasn't always obvious. Four ancient medicine men had been with him since birth and Talks to the Wind started showing up around the age of fifteen. Chris accepted this part of his life as normal just as he accepted his height or hair color.

"How am I supposed to know who they are? I show up and see a beautiful lady by the creek in the first light of day. Then you are taking a leak by this tractor, and I think, hey, this must be Chris's new mate. And I don't understand how but you scored a good woman."

"Excuse me. I was not urinating when you arrived."

"I know my own eyes. It is no matter. You waited until she was away down the bank. I don't know all your ways of this day and age, but I understand men and women take care of the personal stuff in private."

"Can we discuss modern customs another time?" Chris's patience was evaporating rapidly. He stared hard at the fence and spotted a different gap between a section of chain link and the brick building next door. The space appeared wide enough to squeeze through.

"What?" Talks to the Wind asked innocently, yet a hint of accusation was obvious. "You don't think I have anywhere else to be? I have stuff, you know. I stay by your side because you need me. Why else would I be here?"

Chris changed tactics on a whim. Not that anything really happened spontaneously with Chris. He always made decisions from careful thought, even if those thoughts raced at lightning speed. "Can you watch those men for me and tell me what they're doing?"

"Whoa there, brother. I don't think so." He shook his head. "Don't you feel the power rising from our Earth Mother? I won't step my moccasins any closer than where we stand. It's not in my good health. I can't believe my spirit doctor would ask such a thing."

That's it. Chris's patience ran out. Keeping his face neutral as to not let his spirit guide see his lack of staying power, he stared past Talks to the Wind at the men unloading tools and supplies from the back of their truck. Chris thought now was as good a time as any to leave unobserved.

The time he wasted with Talks to the Wind allowed the sun to rise a few degrees. The sky was closer to gray than black, and Chris could see all the way across the lot now. He continued to utilize the fox medicine and visualized himself blending in with the ground and the brick building next door.

To his dismay, Talks to the Wind stayed on Chris's heels. "What are you doing out here? Why aren't you home sleeping by the fire?"

Chris focused on the fence ahead and ignored his tail. The gap was narrower than he first thought. He shot a glance down the fence line at the open gate, but that would be too obvious. Even using the fox medicine, he thought he pushed the limit by walking in plain sight. Daylight had not quite arrived, but the ash gray light brightened by the minute. He shoved the fencepost aside giving him an extra inch, flinched at the clink of the chain links, and slipped through the gap. Sly as a fox sneaking out of the hen house, he vanished into the deeper shadow of a doorway in the condemned building. Chris stilled his breath and listened. Talks to the Wind stopped the chitchat and appeared to be on the lookout, watching around the corner. Perhaps his guide had arrived for a reason after all.

The spirit guide shook his head in a dismissive way. “Didn’t hear a thing. They’re shoveling dirt. That is going to get them nowhere fast. Too much water is flowing out of there. They need to fire up that machinery. Wait.” Talks to the Wind leaned forward, squinting into the gloom. “One of them is headed over to where we were just standing. He’s climbing inside the big machine. The other one jumped down into the ditch.”

Chris heard enough. His truck was parked one door down, and he was doubly glad it was not directly in front of the lot. Naomi still didn't reappear. He refused to worry about her. She found him with no forewarning. She wouldn’t listen when he told her to leave. If she followed the creek downstream, maybe she would meet him on the street. Who knew? That was what he would have done in her shoes. Staying close to the building, he hurried down the sidewalk and jumped inside his pickup, careful not to slam the door. Talks to the Wind sat beside him in the cab.

"Will you find Naomi? Then come back and tell me where she is."

"I told you I cannot get any closer to the vortex. It is like the negative pole of a magnet pushing me away."

Chris sighed and stuck his key in the ignition. Arguing with a spirit, especially *this* spirit, was an exercise in futility.

"I saw the look you gave me," he said. "You don't understand my predicament. It's dangerous out there. I am an enlightened being." Talks to the Wind stared out the windshield toward the construction site and sighed. "For you, my brother, I'll go and take a look. But I may tell her to find a man who doesn't let his woman wander off alone."

Chris's jaw tightened as he strained not to succumb to the goading. Talks to the Wind had to be his least favorite guide, and he didn't fully comprehend why Great Spirit continued to push this relationship on him.

Talks to the Wind grinned wide enough to split his round face. "You never laugh at my jokes. It makes me want to stop trying so hard."

"Your efforts are wasted on me," Chris said truthfully. He also noted that Talks to the Wind continued to sit in the truck rather than do what Chris asked.

"Your lack of humor is funny for one of us. You should see your face right now. I think you would crack like a stone if you ever tried to smile."

"Can you find Naomi now?"

"One smile first. Come on. I'm sure you can do it."

Chris was starting to hate this guy. It took a lot to move Chris to such an extreme emotion. Talks to the Wind was reaching a level of annoyance Chris hadn't experienced in a long time. *Why didn't Naomi just show herself, or come out from wherever she was?*

"You laughed one time. You were seventeen years old. I bet Great Spirit marked the event on his moon calendar."

"Get out," Chris said dryly.

"I'll go, but only because I need to get away from the power surge. It's stronger now."

Talks to the Wind disappeared from the passenger seat. Chris leaned back and hoped the tinted windows and the last of the morning dimness kept him hidden. He pulled out his cell phone and considered reporting his suspicions to his friend at the police department, Officer Howe. Errol Howe trusted and respected Chris's opinion, but not everyone at the sheriff's department did. Unless there was an obvious crime being committed, Chris generally only spoke to Errol. He slid the phone into his vest pocket and waited one last minute for Naomi.

Chris's intuition never failed him. If he actually bothered to listen rather than silently curse Talks to the Wind's existence, he would have heard his gut telling him to start the engine and get out of there ten minutes earlier. Instead, he startled as someone tapped on his window. Before he had a chance to respond, the door yanked open, and Chris's world went black.

Chapter Three

GHOST HUNTER? What had she been thinking? Naomi was experiencing serious regrets about her decision to seek out this guy's help. If there was one thing in the world she couldn't handle, it was the undead. And there Chris stood, last night at the billiard hall. A man who specialized in the field of ghosts, spirits, and the unexplainable. Chris Abeyta arrived late last night at the request of her manager. He and his assistant were supposed to rid the place of rather a mischievous and crafty ghost.

Uh-uh. No way. No how. If she knew Jack's was haunted, she never would have applied for a job. Naomi's travel expenses had been higher than she anticipated and she needed quick cash. Cocktail waitressing at a pool hall fit the bill. Plus, Jack and his manager, Lou — short for Louise — paid under the table. Naomi appreciated the cash without having to fuss over paperwork. She didn't intend to stay in town long, so what was the point in making her employment official.

There had been no problems regarding the supernatural during her first week. She served drinks and delivered bottles of beer and baskets of fries to the pool players. During her fifth night on the job, she decided that spending a month or two in the mountain town would be a great experience. She could save up a few bucks, repair her car, and head to the desert in search of the next energy vortex when the snow started piling up. She was content with her decision and feeling comfortable at her new job. The last thing Naomi ever expected was to be smack-dab in the middle of an episode of *Paranormal Adventures*, or whatever the popular ghost hunting television shows were called. She wouldn't know. Naomi refused to watch anything that freaked her out. It was all too real for her and would cause months of nightmares. *No, thank you.*

A couple of hours after she clocked in for the night, the cook began accusing the bartender and waitresses of stealing food and rearranging the prep table. No one knew a thing about it. Soon after, the cook entered the walk-in cooler, and the shelves emptied themselves onto the floor. He exited the cooler and found every kitchen knife in the room standing on end above the counter as if gravity no longer existed. Carlos shared a few choice words and decided he no longer needed the job. Lou called the owner, Jack. Then her manager dialed some "ghost hunter" who lived in town, and Chris Abeyta arrived shortly after that.

Naomi steered clear of the kitchen excitement and tried to ignore the hushed whispers passing between her bartender and her manager, but she caught the gist of it. She considered offering to help, but ghosts really weren't her forte. Naomi could cast a spell for protection, and she could probably rid the building of one misplaced ghost, but she didn't want to. The heart attack moments and the dangers involved were not worth it. Her craft was more suited to love and abundance potions. She could help someone stay focused and centered during an important interview or test. She could cure a headache and call the deer into the yard. If you wanted singing birds during your wedding ceremony, call Naomi. Expelling unwanted spirits? Out of her wheelhouse. Way out — like located in another universe.

Jack arrived before Chris and his assistant, Juliana. Her boss bravely entered the kitchen and shut down the grill for the night, and he managed to remain uninjured. Lou begged Naomi to stay and take care of the customers before she even had the chance to ask for an early out. Being the new girl, and in desperate need of money, she didn't have a lot of choice in the matter.

In her mind, if she left work, she would be totally alone — and alone with a ghost seemed a lot worse than with a group of living, breathing people. Since she currently slept in her camper trailer behind Jack's, the proximity of her mobile home was too close for comfort. Better to remain with the herd and be informed.

So, she stayed. Naomi cast a spell around herself to remain unseen unless she wanted to be seen. The magic she called upon used air and light waves. A technique learned at a young age. Bending light and shifting air currents proved useful in many circumstances, including confusing wayward spirits.

As she took care of the customers, Naomi had been thoroughly fascinated with how the Native American shaman worked his magic. His power came from a source foreign to her, and it appeared to come easily. Apparently, no fancy implements were needed. A commanding voice, some sage, and sweetgrass, and not much else. From what little she caught, his technique was otherworldly. The feelings he elicited within her bubbled, new and thrilling. Naomi was awestruck.

Just before Naomi served last call, the ghost hunter, and his assistant, finished up and left the pool hall. She shepherded the late night stragglers out the door, collected the rest of her tips, bussed a couple tables, and said goodnight to Lou, Jack, and her bartender.

Living behind her place of employment had become a necessary inconvenience due to the engine light glowing orange on the dashboard of her old Subaru. The light came on over a month ago. She didn't have enough money for the repair. Leaking oil and black smoke aside, the car continued to run. She suspected that was only due to the number of prayers and spells she kept in her prayer grid.

Inside her travel trailer, she could not calm the apprehension buzzing through her insides. Something felt amiss, a supernatural disturbance in the air that had not been there before. Naomi lit candles, incense, and rearranged the crystals and stones in her prayer grid, but nothing made a difference. If she was going to find any peace, she needed to move her car and trailer away from Jack's Corner Pocket. She could park for the night just outside of town in the national forest and wake up in the morning surrounded by the serenity of the woods.

Naomi looked at her magic circle made of quartz and amethyst crystals. The pyramid and other geometric patterns inside the circle glowed with a soft iridescence, confirming its positive charge. She held her palms over the circle and focused her mind. The folded notes and prayers overflowed the circle. With a dubious look, she realized she would need to invest in some larger crystals soon if she continued to pile on the spells and prayers inside the grid.

Leaning over from her spot on the edge of her bed, she grabbed a small notebook and wrote, "I'm safe from all harm." "My Subie runs perfectly," and, "I have more money than I need." She tore the affirmations from the pad, folded them into squares, and placed them on top of all the other requests. Naomi blew out her candles, grabbed her incense, and stepped out of the trailer and into her car. She stuck the burning stick of incense in the ashtray and started the engine. The motor turned over and she stared at the orange light requesting maintenance. Naomi sent some positive thoughts to her magic grid, and then shifted into drive. It's the last thing she remembered before seeing Chris, the ghost hunter, sleeping in bed.

* * *

Now she found herself watching two men drag Chris from his truck. He was inert and looking like this wasn't the best morning of his life. Who were these guys? Why did they hurt Chris? He was just sitting in his truck minding his own business. Okay, maybe that wasn't one hundred percent true. They'd both been snooping around. She didn't think they saw him, but she was too busy trying to puzzle out why this location projected so much Earth energy. And she had been attempting to measure the vortex. Her extrasensory perception told her the vortex was expanding rapidly. A phenomenon she had never heard of before.

The construction workers didn't scare her away from exploring along the creek. The men were obviously preoccupied with the trench and the leaking pipe. She stayed out of sight, and the men never glanced her way. The ghost dressed like a time traveling Native American gave her the heebie-jeebies, though. She caught him spying on her, and he looked overly interested in what she was doing. The goofy look on his face didn't match the intensity in his eyes, and well, the whole dead thing had her scurrying away from finding the borders of the vortex. She decided it was time to find Chris. He was the paranormal specialist after all, and he could take care of the oddball creeper following her.

Naomi dragged a hand over her scalp and tugged at her curls. She couldn't believe the men were kidnapping Chris. She thought they were harmless only a few minutes earlier. What the heck had happened while she investigated the vortex? She glanced over her shoulder for like the tenth time. The Native American ghost had disappeared — *thank the Goddess.* Naomi hid behind the excavator, waiting and watching.

"Dude, why did you hit this guy?"

"He was trespassing. I smelled something shifty about him. Take a look at this blowhole. I bet he works for the city. An inspector, or worse, code enforcement."

"You screwed up bad, man. You're going to be in deep shit with the boss over this."

"We're not telling him squat. Besides, he's my dad. He won't fire me."

"You're walking a fine line, Todd. After you hit his car with the backhoe last week, he said that was your last mistake. You're so done."

"Shut up. I am not. You have to help me dump this cocksucker."

"Seriously? You're an asshole, you know that."

"It takes one to know one. Listen, Marlin," Todd said. "We're here to fix a problem, and that's what I'm going to do, but first, we tie and gag this loser, drive him out to Tim-buk-fucking-tu, and by the time he resurfaces in town, we'll have this covered up. No one will know a thing."

"Who ties your shoes for you in the morning? That is the worst plan I've ever heard. You're going to get us both fired, you stupid shit."

"Oh, yeah? Then why are you helping me?"

"Because, Todd,"

The man drew out Todd's name with a patronizing tone that made Naomi's spine itch.

He went on. "Since you took it upon yourself to cold-cock this dude, without finding out who he is or what he's doing here, we don't have many options left."

Marlin dropped Chris's legs and opened the back door on their quad cab truck.

"So you're saying I'm right. We gotta get him out of here before anyone spots us."

"You're not right. You're a dumbass. And yeah, let's get him out of sight. Where's the duct tape?" He leaned into the truck.

Naomi stared hard as he rifled through the detritus on the backseat. Seconds later, he bound Chris with the tape. The two men lacked grace or care in every way as they hefted Chris into the truck and slammed the door.

Naomi winced in empathy for Chris's unmoving body. What was she going to do now?

Todd walked around to the driver's side and pulled open the door. "Marlin! What are you doing? Let's get out of here."

Marlin stopped walking toward the skid steer and backtracked. "We have to fix the mess you made yesterday. It's almost daylight. If anyone sees the water running, and the pipes you broke and reports it, we're in deep shit. The city will be all over us. The building department, EPA, city planner, and the freaking mayor will be all up in our business. You know how anal they are about every stupid thing, but especially their mineral hot springs. Your father will be fined, ticketed, and ordered to pay for God knows what."

"They'll want him to replace every inch of rusted pipeline for the entire town while the tree hugging assholes count every bug and bunny in the county," Todd said.

"We should have fixed this yesterday when you realized how badly you screwed up the job. Who digs in the wrong spot? You need to learn how to follow directions," Marlin whisper-yelled.

"Did you forget to take your Midol this morning or what?"

"Go screw yourself."

"Don't have to. I already got some last night. Which is why I didn't want to work in this mud hole until after dark yesterday. Maybe that's your problem. You're not getting enough."

"Shut your damn trap, and help me finish this. Then we can take care of your *other* problem." Marlin stomped across the lot and climbed into the skid steer. The engine growled to life, coughing and sputtering exhaust into the chill autumn air.

"Whatever," Todd complained. "He won't be going anywhere." Todd left the truck door open and returned to work. When he reached the trench, he picked up a discarded shovel and leaned against it. Marlin ground the skid loader into gear and resumed pushing dirt into the trench.

Naomi didn't waste another second. She snuck into the cab through the open door and climbed over the console to the back seat. Chris's eyes opened wide, and he grunted against the tape over his mouth.

"Fancy meeting you here," she said. "I wouldn't have pictured you for kink, but you know, to each their own," she said, nonchalant and inappropriately making light of the situation.

Chris rewarded her with a glare through narrowed eyes. He could almost pull off an Asian face when he did that. She considered telling him that he'd make a decent looking Korean if his eyes permanently squinted like that, but held in the observation. It wasn't PC. These days, everyone seemed to get offended by just about anything, plus she didn't think Chris would appreciate her thoughts just now, given the circumstances. With desperation and panic driving her movements, she tried peeling the tape off his ankles and didn't make much progress. He shook his head with urgency while mumbling something incoherent.

"Alright, but I'm going to do it fast." He wore the squinty face again as she reached over to remove the duct tape from his mouth. Yep, definitely looked Asian when he made that face. Her Korean mother would approve.

Her mother may be Korean, but she married a Native American and African American U.S. Army soldier. Naomi grew up listening to comments about finding a nice Korean man, even though her own mother did not. *What was with that?* She and her mother had opposite views on just about every topic of discussion, but no more stridently than about who she should and should not date. In Naomi's opinion, sexual and mental attraction had absolutely nothing to do with ethnicity and everything to do with butterflies and goose bumps. Chills ran up and down her arms when she looked Chris in the eyes, and she didn't know what to make of it.

She picked at the tape on his cheek until she had a firm grip on the edge and ripped. Every muscle in his body tensed and the muscles of his jaw hardened. To her surprise, he remained silent as he breathed through the free hair removal technique.

"There's a knife in my vest pocket," he said through gritted teeth. Then unnecessarily added, "Hurry."

She patted around his waist and chest and didn't find anything resembling a knife. However, she did enjoy a good feel of rock hard abs. For a lean man, he had some nice muscle tone. Chris caught on to her predicament.

"My inside left pocket."

"Okay." She searched again, and a surge of intimacy rushed through her bloodstream. This was the most intimate she had been with a man in forever. Too bad he had to be tied up. She kept her face hidden behind her hair as she dug around the bottom of the pocket and fished out the folding knife. With deft hands, she sliced through the tape with ease.

"Wow, sharp knife," she commented.

Chris sat up, and she squeezed around him to place the knife at a good angle to cut the tape binding his wrists. Unfortunately, she glanced over at Todd and Marlin and saw something she could never imagine in her worst nightmares.

The thugs were busy working on the trench and ditches. Todd actually used the shovel instead of leaning on it, and Marlin continued to operate the skid steer. What freaked her out beyond comprehension was the circling vortex of energy funneling over the construction site and the arrival of at least thirty members of the undead. She knew they weren't alive because of their semi-transparency. Some of the ghosts circled around with the funnel cloud of pure Earth energy, while others hovered or lingered near Todd and the open end of the trench.

"That's what I was afraid of," Chris said. "Ow!" He yanked his hands out of the way.

Naomi shook like she was on permanent vibrate and accidentally cut him. He plucked the knife from her hand and snapped it shut. It went into his vest pocket, and he inspected the cut on his arm. Only a nick.

"Sorry."

"I'll live. Let's get out of here."

"You do see that, don't you? What is it? What's going on?" She babbled, scrambling away as fast as possible.

Outside of the truck, every ghost turned their eyes on them. All the blood in her body seemed to drain away. A black velvet shroud clouded her vision, and she swayed. Chris grabbed a hold of her and flashed a look of intolerance. She had the wherewithal to realize how easily she read his expression, even though they just met. She thought it was kind of funny, considering how he kept his expressions neutral. Being adept at empathy, she was used to knowing how the people around her felt and sensing their moods, but she was clearly reading his facial features. If she weren't about to pee her pants with fright she'd like to share with him what a ripe turd he was for making faces at her.

Todd screamed, and she jolted back to the present. Passing out would have been so much better. Instead, she threw a glance behind them. Two ghosts stole Todd's shovel. Naomi watched the shovel fly through the air and land somewhere over the sloped embankment that led to the creek. The skid loader wheeled around, and the engine died. The lot went silent. Another ghost climbed inside the cab with Marlin. The female spirit braced herself against the steel frame of the cab, lifted a leg and kicked Marlin off the seat with a booted heel. He tumbled out of the machine and landed in the dirt. Neither man could possibly be wearing clean shorts after the ghostly attack. Naomi barely controlled her own bladder as she and Chris made a break for it.

"What the hell!" she heard behind them.

"How did he bust out of the truck?"

"Grab him!"

"What do you think I'm doing!"

Naomi and Chris flew toward the pickup truck and threw themselves inside. She watched in horror as ghosts flocked behind and above Todd and Marlin.

One lithe male ghost materialized in front of Todd and screamed, “Don’t take away our vortex!”

Todd hit the sidewalk and rolled. He cowered, covering his head with beefy arms as he curled up like a baby. Marlin stopped and picked up his coworker. This gave Chris the time he needed to start the truck and tear away from the freak show.

Yeah, he was a ghost hunter, but come on, that didn’t mean he would always be surrounded by the nonliving, did it? *Wow, she was on a roll.* She just couldn’t figure out when she became a frequent flyer of the Bad Decisions Club.

“You know what, Chris? I would hang out with you a lot more if it were always this exciting,” Talks to the Wind said.

When the dead Indian appeared between them, spoke, and grinned at her, Naomi jumped so high she hit her head on the ceiling. After she finished screeching, she gripped her chest and passed out.

Chapter Four

"SHE'S A JUMPY ONE. Maybe you should teach her the ways of spirit."

Chris tried a steadying breath. It failed miserably. Anxiety and irritation wouldn't be alleviated with one well-intentioned inhale. While continuing to take long slow breaths he silently asked Great Spirit for clarity, fortitude, and the ability to endure through the morning. Better yet, he should request a new personality. His wasn't working for him. He was on the verge of banishing Talks to the Wind to the farthest unknown reaches of the netherworld and taking pleasure doing it.

"What happened back there? In all my winters, I have never seen such a thing as what lay behind us. It is as if the Great Mother split open and pours out her life force."

"That about sums it up," Chris replied. "The new vortex is attracting lost souls and errant spirits."

"It is pushing me away," Talks to the Wind said.

"You are not lost or wayward," Chris pointed out.

"That is a thought."

A rumble or vibration in the air like that of a loud diesel engine had him checking his rearview mirror.

What he saw upped his anxiety. The men who attacked him rounded the corner in their truck, tires squealing in pursuit. Chris pressed the gas pedal and took the next left at high speed. The truck leaned hard, pushing the suspension to its limit, and tossed Naomi into the door.

She moaned and came to. A good thing, he thought, although gently nudging her would have been a nicer way to wake her. Her eyelids flickered and then spread wide with fright when she saw Talks to the Wind sitting beside her.

"No more screaming," he said as her mouth dropped open with a little pop.

"I don't bite," Talks to the Wind assured.

Her mouth shut, then opened again. Repeatedly.

"Let me give her a new name. Fish Face suits her," Talks to the Wind said. "Look at those lips sucking air."

Chris saw the resemblance. This was not the clarity he asked for from Great Spirit. He'd been referring to a clear understanding of why he was led to the construction site, why the land was so off balance, and how to bring harmony back to his mountain town. The way Naomi's eyes bulged with fright, she resembled one of those goldfish with protruding eyes.

Chris gave Talks to the Wind a shrug. "Fish Face." He tried the name out for himself. He didn't agree or disagree aloud. Although, it did fit. "You should leave now. You're scaring my guest. If you get rid of my tail, I'll let you name her whatever you like."

Talks to the Wind glanced over his shoulder. The workers continued to hound them.

"I'll see what I can do."

Chris didn't count on him being of much help regarding the thugs. But his spirit guide leaving would help improve Naomi's color and overall health.

In the rearview mirror, he watched the truck come to an abrupt stop. The driver's side door flew open, and the driver jumped out and appeared to be smacking himself. Chris thought he saw smoke and caught a glimpse of Talks to the Wind in the cab with the other man. He lost sight of the trio as he turned right on another back street.

"You lost them." Naomi finally found her voice.

"Maybe," he said.

"Can we go to Jack's Corner Pocket now?"

"That's where I'm headed."

* * *

The truck lurched as Chris turned into the parking lot of the billiard hall. The high speed wouldn't have been as much a problem if not for the car and mini camper blocking half the driveway.

Naomi sat with her neck craned around on the lookout for their pursuers. She bobbed up and down hanging onto the emergency handle as the pickup bounced across the lot.

"Whoa there, cowboy!" she whooped as Chris swerved around the camper trailer and hit a pothole roughly the size of the Grand Canyon. "Professional ghost hunters should know how to drive, don't cha' think?"

He slid her the side eye. "My driving is fine. I can't say the same about the parking abilities of Ms. Green Subaru back there."

Naomi scratched her head. "Hey, I drive a green Subaru," she said sounding offended. "I'm sure bouncing around has nothing to do with the color green."

She glanced back. Chris had already wheeled around the building and steered into a parking space out of sight of the road and the green Subaru wagon and trailer. Parking in the back was all he could do for now. He would just hope he'd lost the men in the pickup truck for good. He wondered if, or when, Talks to the Wind would return with an update. Chris never knew when his guide would make an appearance. He often called to his other spirit guides when he wanted help. Talks to the Wind was unpredictable and sporadic at best.

"I'm assuming you can get us inside," he said as they hurried to the back door of Jack's.

"I guess I can," she said with a shrug.

"I don't have a key," he said flatly. "And I do not think anyone would be inside at this time of morning."

"Right, but I *do* have a key."

"How come I did not see you last night?" he asked.

"I was hiding from you. I'm not a fan of ghosts and the like."

"I noticed. You realize the irony don't you?"

"Hush," she scolded and narrowed an eye at him. "I can't help myself."

"I would bet against that statement."

"Do you want to go inside or not?" she said, still huffy about him pointing out her personality flaw of being overly sensitive towards members of the nonliving. Naomi turned the knob and pushed the door open but didn't enter.

Chris reached forward and held the door. "After you."

"No thanks. You go ahead of me, champ."

"Scared of ghosts," he mumbled and gave a not quite concealed disapproving shake of his head. He walked in and flipped the light switch.

"The lights aren't working?" Naomi's panic made her voice go up an octave.

"Electrical disturbances are common in circumstances like these."

"I don't bloody care. I'm out of here." Naomi made to retreat even though she'd only stepped one foot inside the door.

Chris debated with himself. Was it better to let her remain outside and out of his way, or did he need her to stay close by? "You came to me for help. If you want it, you need to stay with me."

The internal battle registered on her stricken face. Chris reached into his vest and pulled out his keychain flashlight.

"Please tell me that's a ghost zapping laser?" she asked hopefully.

Why did he suddenly think he was the butt of some cosmic joke orchestrated by Great Spirit? He blinked at Naomi, clicked on the flashlight, and proceeded down the dim hallway. Daylight streamed in from behind them until the door swung closed. Naomi practically landed on top of him after the loud bang. He cleared his throat and glanced over his shoulder. She clung to his vest and became the monkey on his back — literally. As much as he wanted to, he did not insist she give him some space. The woman would probably pass out again, and he didn't need the holdup. Chris directed the beam of light down the dark hallway until it reached the filtered light coming through an open doorway on the right.

"The kitchen," she breathed in his ear.

"Whispering is unnecessary, Naomi. We're alone. If we aren't, we don't want to surprise anyone — living or nonliving," Chris said in his normal voice.

What he refrained from saying was that the vibrational shift inside Jack's was significantly different since he had been there last night. Chris ventured forward seeking out the cause of the change. He felt the energetic vacuum all the way to the marrow of his bones. He reviewed the events of the previous night and realized how focused he had been on removing the impish spirit. What he neglected was the foundation and the grounds around the pool hall. He turned into the kitchen and had a moment of clarity. The offending spirit had purposefully distracted him from a more complex case.

"I missed something last night," he murmured to himself.

Running on little sleep and having a woman clinging to his back, Chris realized his focus was not as sharp as it should be. He tried to pull himself together and only half succeeded. The entire aura of Jack's had shifted in only a few hours. This disturbed him even more than the thought that the ghost tricked him. Jack's Corner Pocket did not have the feeling of a bottomless chasm last night. He would have noticed. Not only did it feel like the ground was sucking him down, but a slight sense of vertigo hovered in the periphery. His personal energy level was too high to be consumed by the negativity of the building. A layperson or average Joe — someone who knew nothing of energetic protection — would become ill if they spent more than a few minutes here. Chris couldn't ignore the situation to go catch up on sleep and come back later when he was refreshed.

Jack needed an update. Chris pulled out his phone and tapped the power button. The phone didn't wake up. He tried a second time and the screen remained black. Electronic devices couldn't handle the frequencies overwhelming the building. As strong as it was, he would be surprised if his phone ever worked again.

"That's not good," Naomi pointed out over his shoulder.

"Everything will be fine." Chris deposited the phone back in his pocket.

"Did you say you forgot to do something last night?" she asked.

He shone the light around the darkened kitchen. One high narrow window along the sidewall provided daylight. The stainless steel countertops and appliances blended in with the gray light turning the room into a nondescript and dreary box.

"Yes. I'm not sure what it is. I spent most of my time in the billiard room, smoking room, and the attic. I saw the kitchen briefly. Is there an office?"

He made his way around the kitchen shining the flashlight over every surface, including the baseboards, ceiling, and walls.

"There's an office by the front counter, and there are two storage rooms. One for kitchen and restaurant supplies and one for billiard and janitor supplies." She continued to whisper.

"Show me where they are."

Naomi shook her head, refusing.

"The sooner we find the source of the problem, the sooner we solve *your* mystery."

After what felt like hours had passed, she averted her gaze to a short hallway in the corner of the kitchen. A restroom sign hung next to one door, but he made out another closed door.

Where other people would be repelled, Chris was drawn to the back of the kitchen like iron filings to a magnet. His intuition flared. He found what he sought.

"I'll wait over here," Naomi said.

Chris swung the door open and leaned in, but didn't enter the storeroom. Something akin to trepidation rose to the forefront of his awareness. A rare occurrence for the normally unflappable shaman. A frisson swept over his skin raising the fine hairs on the back of his neck and arms. "I thought this might be the case." He stared at the unstable energetic mass. "Jack's pool hall is located in direct opposition to the vortex on Hermosa Ave."

The energy vortex definitely had not been inside the storeroom last night. It had to have formed after he left. As he stood there, the vortex expanded. Its spiraling center lay well beneath the floor buried within the Earth. In his mind, Chris visualized the underground rivers and passageways of the water table. Jack's Corner Pocket had to be located on top of, or very close to, potent geothermal activity. Chris would bet money that the coordinates of this vortex aligned with the vortex on

Hermosa Ave. Naomi edged closer, straining to see around Chris.

"Do you think this has anything to do with your confusion?" he asked.

Energetic fields aren't always visible. Some adepts feel them. Some only sense them with their third eye, and some people, like him, see them just as clearly as the shelves lined up against the walls.

"I think we're in deep doo-doo," Naomi said, retreating from the storage room.

"That did not go as well as I planned," Talks to the Wind said behind her.

Naomi whirled around. Chris reacted before she had a chance to scream or pass out.

He clapped a hand over her mouth. "Don't scream. He is with me. Just like you are." He strategically placed himself between Talks to the Wind and Naomi.

"Fish Face is still on the nervous side. Haven't you figured out her deal yet?"

Staying focused on Naomi required most of his attention. If she passed out again, he would be stuck in the kitchen until she regained consciousness. They didn't have time for that. He removed his hand from her mouth. "Take deep breaths and keep looking at me. Talks to the Wind is my spirit guide, and he's here to help... if you can call it helping. That point is debatable." He said this last bit more to himself than her. "Can you hear me, Naomi?" He gave her a little shake.

She nodded almost imperceptively but continued to stare into his eyes. Chris boosted her energy level by sending some of his life force energy into her through eye contact. He breathed deep and adjusted his energetic vibration to be calm and centered. The method worked, and her panic subsided.

"What is going on?" Chris asked his guide.

Talks to the Wind leaned out the kitchen door and peered down the hallway. "I came ahead of them to give you some time, but your woman is high maintenance. Now there is no time."

"I know there is not enough time," he said, frustrated. "What are you talking about, Talks to the Wind? In case you do not feel it, there's a cataclysmic energetic void that must be dealt with."

"They're here. The two uglies and a boat load — well, it is actually a truckload — of displaced spirits. I gotta get out of this weird place. It's sucking me in," Talks to the Wind said and disappeared.

Chris grabbed Naomi's hand and pulled her out of the kitchen. "Time to go."

She gasped with surprise when he yanked her across the room. They dashed into the hall just in time to see the back door of Jack's swing open and hear Todd and Marlin arguing.

"What the hell is happening?"

"They're freaking dead! All of them! Just do what they say!"

"I don't believe in ghosts!"

"Ow! One just hit me."

"This is crazy. It's not possible!" Marlin argued.

"I don't know, man, but they brought us here, and that's our guy's truck in the parking lot. I'm going to find him and wring the bastard's neck. He's doing this. I'm sure of it. And I'm not getting busted for a mistake."

"Your dad is going to fire your ass, and mine too."

"Shut up, man. Let's just find him."

"Look! The ghosts are leaving us alone now."

Naomi darted in front Chris and started dragging him farther into the building.

"Where are we going?" Chris whispered as they entered the nearly pitch black pool hall.

"I'm getting you out of here."

"How?"

They zigged and zagged around the pool tables, cue racks, support beams, and chairs. Chris could barely see Naomi in front of him, but he trusted that she knew her way across the large room. They veered left, and he spotted an emergency exit sign. Chris reached out to push the door open, but as soon as daylight streaked inside, he saw a throng of ghosts waiting for someone to open the door. They sneered at him with distorted faces. These were not garden-variety lost souls. They appeared demented and full of malice. He slammed the door and threw up a wall of spiritual protection by raising his hands and saying a prayer in his native tongue.

"More friends of yours?" Naomi said as she started in another direction.

With the flash of daylight, he got a glimpse of the billiard hall. They could skirt down the length of the room toward the smoking lounge. If he remembered correctly, the smoking club had its own exit.

"Not this time," Chris said as they hurried across the room.

"He's in here!" Todd called out.

"Who? More ghosts?"

"No, you idiot. Our escape artist."

Chris wouldn't turn his flashlight on. The dark gave him a better chance of getting out unnoticed. Plus, he was proficient in moving without making any sound. That is until he collided with a chair.

A grunt of pain erupted out of him as he cracked his shin, stumbled, and went down in a tangle of wooden legs. Back on his feet in the next second, he heard Todd or Marlin catching up with him. He silently cursed himself a thousand ways to Sunday as he hopped on one foot and continued to move forward.

"Over here," he heard in his ear.

Without warning, Naomi grasped his arm and pulled him aside.

Stunned by her maneuver, he didn't make any real attempt to free himself. Her hand was on him and making him move. The reality of her action didn't sit well with him. Not that anything that happened this morning did.

Naomi shoved him against the wall, but there was no wall. He stumbled into a closet or cubby space. They sunk into soft coats and jackets and she arranged them as a screen. Before he had the chance to orient himself, Naomi pressed her lips to his. *What?* Not only did she put her hands on him, but now she was kissing him. Chris yanked his head away from her extraordinarily warm and soft, but intrusive, lips to gawk at her. *Did Chris gawk?* He couldn't remember ever doing so before. Not that she could see him in the dark, but gawking?

"Play along, Silly-Billy, or they're going to see you," she murmured.

"They are going to see us anyway."

"No, they won't. Trust me on this. No one will see you around this massive set of curls. And all the coats." He heard the smile in her whisper.

She had a point, he thought. Her hair could shield just about anything smaller than a Mack truck. Before he came up with an alternative plan to hiding behind Naomi's 'fro, she laid her lips against his again. The magic she threw around them was unlike anything he'd experienced before. He instinctively knew she created a shield of protection around them. He suspected she used a type of projected camouflage to distort and hide them. The air vibrated and shimmered. Chris went with it.

He didn't comprehend the impulsiveness. Impulse control was something he excelled at since the day he was born. It might have been the taste of her, apple with a hint of spice. The woman definitely knew how to cover up the tobacco from the cigarette she smoked in his cabin. Not that tobacco really bothered him. He grew up using a ceremonial pipe. Prayers were sent with the smoke for just about any reason his father could come up with — to end the drought, to heal the sick, to ease the passing of a soul, to help his father's cousin Edna win at bingo. Tobacco had a unique sweetness in the medicine pipe, and now it had a unique flavor on Naomi's playful lips.

The cramped closet turned quite cozy as Chris closed the gap between them. He palmed her back and pressed her body against the length of him. A sound resembling a purr vibrated out of Naomi. Teeth grazed his lower lip, and she leaned hard against him. Primal urges came few and far between for Chris — at least where his sex drive was concerned. His abdomen clenched all the way down to his groin. He ran an exploratory hand along her spine, over her shoulder, and cupped her head in his hand as he deepened the kiss. Their tongues met and twined. Her hands trailed down his sides and gripped his waist. Naomi's heartbeat picked up, beating against his chest like a drum.

How? He kept asking himself. How was Naomi doing any of this? How did she light a cigarette? How had she manifested a physical body so quickly and released it just as fast?

Spirits can move physical objects. This is a well-known fact. But it takes the average spirit a fair amount of natural talent, a lot of practice, and immense control. Naomi's supernatural abilities were blowing his mind. What kind of otherworldly apparition was she? He had to find out as soon as possible. Making out with a spirit had never happened before. It had to be wrong, even if he presently liked it. Her evasiveness regarding exactly who she was and what she was doing here would not cut the mustard for much longer.

"Damn it! I lost them," Todd said.

"We need to get out of here. You're going to get us arrested," Marlin said.

"No. That spying little punk is here, and I'm not leaving without him."

Naomi broke the kiss. He all but felt her gaze lingering on his mouth. They listened to the two men move away from their closet. Crashing sounds echoed around the room as if Todd and Marlin collided with pool tables and a chair or two.

"This is crap. I'm outta here," Marlin called.

Chris could tell Marlin was on the far side of the room.

"That's enough tonsil hockey for now." Naomi patted his chest and spun around, placing her back against him. Her fluffy hair tickled the underside of his chin before she released her physical form. Naomi was back in her spirit body. Chris longed to know more about her and the magic she used. She wasn't dead, that much he knew. Her spirit was still tied to her physical body somewhere. But where? Where was she and why was she out of body? Astral projection could be a dangerous undertaking. Why was she doing it so haphazardly? Naomi slid out from the coats.

When he didn't move to follow, she leaned back in. "Don't pout, sport. We can commence canoodling later."

Chris registered the jibe and shook off the hormonal haze. Just as he was about to follow her, the metal door handle creaked, and a wash of daylight spread across the room.

Marlin held the emergency door open. Chris saw his seal of protection break, bursting like a popped bubble. It had not been a permanent seal, given that he created it in seconds and only with a simple prayer and a small, focused burst of energy.

"If you leave me alone in this haunted place I'll tell the cops you were the one who hit that blowhole and shoved him inside the truck," Todd said.

That grabbed both Marlin and Chris's attention. It was both a good and a bad thing that Marlin opened the door. Good because Chris saw that Todd wasn't where he thought he was. He stood near the smoking room. Just where Chris would have gone next. Bad because the spiritual protection broke and the ghosts waiting outside had an open door to enter through.

Naomi froze in place as she stared at Todd. Chris threw his gaze back to Marlin and the open door. Ghosts of all sizes and shapes flew into the billiard hall. One barged into Marlin, knocking him aside. The hefty construction worker screamed in terror, went down on one knee, and then bounced back up. Marlin appeared stricken with some form of self-inflicted mania as he brushed and slapped at his body.

Todd couldn't see Naomi in her spirit form standing almost right in front of him. He did see his friend acting like a lunatic. Naomi must have forgotten she was invisible. She ran to move out of Todd's way. Chris's jaw clenched with frustration as she panicked and ran the wrong direction.

"What in the hell was that?"

"It ran me over. This is crazy! We gotta get out of here!" Marlin cried out as he darted away from the still open door.

As soon as he moved the door swung closed. Chris jumped out of the closet after Naomi and caught up with her a few feet from the hallway leading toward the kitchen. The ghosts also headed that direction, and he knew what would happen as soon as Naomi spotted them.

A blood-curdling scream tore out of her when a ghost rushed past, bumped her, and disappeared into the kitchen.

"Calm down. We're getting out of here right now!" he told her.

"There he is!" Todd yelled after hearing Chris speak.

The mistake couldn't be taken back. He knew it, but Naomi suffered from a crippling fear of ghosts, and he had only been thinking of her when he spoke. He forced her to move toward the back door, but she somehow put on the brakes, and he couldn't move her. Ghosts, hell-bent on finding the vortex in the storage room, poured down the hallway from both directions.

Todd and Marlin were coming at him from the billiard room. Chris had no other option but to leave through the back door at the end of the hall. Nothing in this world would let him leave Naomi behind with these warped and twisted souls. The vortex was creating an unprecedented phenomenon, and it attracted malicious and foul ghosts.

The building creaked and groaned around them. A loud crack came from overhead, and the ceiling seemed to shift. Enough was enough, and Chris took charge of the situation. He picked her up off her feet, spirit to spirit. Astral traveling witch or not, she couldn't resist the immense power of his true self. She clung to him as he sprinted down the hallway. Crashing sounds boomed out of the kitchen and storage room. The building moaned and the paint split and began to crumble. He should not have looked, but he couldn't help himself. The kitchen overflowed with ghosts who looked possessed with rage. He didn't stall or stumble, but as he dashed out the door, he caught a glimpse of Todd being shoved into the kitchen by a horde of frenzied ghosts. As the door swung shut again, Marlin dove into the kitchen after his friend.

* * *

Chris sprinted to the truck. Jack's Corner Pocket screeched and snapped as the southeast corner of the building caved in. He yanked open the driver's side door and jumped inside. Naomi scrambled across the cab to the passenger seat. Her dark chocolate eyes were glued to the disaster, and her whole body trembled.

"Where is your physical body, Naomi?" He needed to get to the bottom of this mystery. Her insistence to come to Jack's made him think she must be here.

"That's a gray area." Her eyes rolled skyward in a half circle as if searching for the answer inside her head.

As she stalled, his patience slipped to a precarious degree. It had been tenuous to start with. "I do not understand 'gray area.' How do you not know where your body is?"

She swallowed and stuck her tongue in her cheek before speaking. "Listen here, bucko. Not everyone has a firm grip on the location of their physical body. I've meant to ask you to help me find it."

Chris's brows drew together. This was new. Everything about Naomi seemed new to him. "Were you in an accident?" He needed to know how urgent her situation was. Things were already bad enough with two hooligans chasing after him and a vortex that needed to be closed before the town was bombarded with energy vampires and wayward spirits.

"Hmm... Well... It's hard to remember."

Her stalling coupled with vague answers compelled Chris to draw in a long calming breath. He tried another tactic. "What is the last thing you remember?"

"Leaving work. Kind of like what we're doing now, except I'm pretty sure it was dark outside."

Chris frowned. "Were you ill?"

"I don't think so."

Her answers didn't help.

"We have to get out of here. Is there any chance you're inside the pool hall?"

Chris nailed the gas pedal and the truck peeled out of the parking space.

"No. I remember leaving for the night and going to my trailer."

As he rounded the building, the truck fishtailed and came within inches of crashing into the camper and Subaru still blocking half of the driveway entrance. He swerved, held his breath, and prayed for a miss. No screech of metal followed, and he gunned the accelerator to high-tail it out of there. Chris chanced a look back. Todd was dragging Marlin from the building.

"They made it out! I can't believe it!" Her gaze was fixed on Jack's. The entire back side of the building fell apart. "Todd needs to go away... like to prison," Naomi added.

"I wish you could call 911 for me," he said as he concentrated on not wrecking the truck as they bounced over potholes.

"I'll ruin your phone if I touch it. My vibe is too powerful for a sensitive device like that."

"I know. I'll call, and then we'll figure out where you are." With one hand gripping the wheel, Chris pulled the phone out of his pocket.

"Come on, come on," he urged as he held down the power button and willed it to wake up. The irony that he actually wanted his electronic leash to be in working condition when he regularly cursed the device for existing at all didn't escape him. At the moment, Chris was both repulsed and grateful for the phone — that is, if it still worked.

He had no idea if his phone survived the close proximity to the vortex. Forever and a day seemed to pass before the screen lit up. He glanced at Naomi and saw she wasn't looking at him, or the phone is his hand, but back at the car and the travel trailer in the driveway.

He glimpsed the Subaru in the rearview mirror and the epiphany struck him like a sledgehammer at the exact same time Naomi said, "That's my car!"

Chris braked, slammed the truck into reverse, and jolted forward as the truck switched directions. He punched in the number for emergency services, turned on the speakerphone, and threw open the door. Naomi and Chris ran toward the Subaru. A dispatcher came on the line and asked what the emergency was. Chris blurted out the address, and a brief description then hung up.

A huge smile spread across Naomi's face. You'd think that all was well in her world, but Chris didn't like what lay before him. Naomi's body was slumped over in the driver's seat. He couldn't tell what was wrong with her.

"You found me!" Naomi planted a smacking kiss on his cheek. "I knew I had the right man for the job."

He found her cheerful response inappropriate given the collapsed building, the horde of unstable ghosts, two irate thugs, and her passed out body. He gave her a stern look.

She revised, even though her happiness didn't waver. "Okay, so maybe I was slightly skeptical for a little while there. I mean you and Mr. Talks to the Wind tried to scare the life out of me, but I shouldn't have doubted. You totally did it. I was right here the whole time. Duh! I'm an idiot."

"Are you sick?"

"No. I think I was driving away, and the vortex opened. The shift was so powerful. I got scared, and I didn't know what to do. Then I was inside your house." She looked both apologetic and surprised by her admission.

Chris cocked a brow and frowned. He reached for the door handle, but it refused to open. "Unlock the door, Naomi," he ordered. "It's time for you to return to your body."

Without answering, she disappeared from his side. He watched her slip into the front seat of the car and back into her body.

"Wake up!" Chris knocked on the window.

She didn't respond. He continued yelling and pounding on the car. He strained to check her breathing and barely saw the rise and fall of her chest. His anxiety lessened a few degrees. But why was she unresponsive? Unintentional, and unprotected, astral travel is extraordinarily dangerous. Without her spirit inside her physical shell, she was vulnerable to walk-ins, possession, and death.

Chris saw her hand twitch. "Naomi!"

Through the screen of her curls, he thought her eyelids wavered. That's when he heard it. The engine roared, and he recognized the sound. Chris looked up in time to see the construction truck round the side of Jack's Corner Pocket. The heavy-duty pickup fishtailed just as Chris's truck had. In his mind's eye, Chris saw the accident coming and threw up a shield of protection. He called for his spirit guides. Talks to the Wind arrived almost instantaneously and shoved Chris aside. His sphere of protection warped, wobbled, and didn't reach out as far as he wanted it to. Chris hit the ground. The back of Todd's truck swung hard to the left, tires throwing up a spray of gravel like a shotgun blast. Todd gunned the engine and overcorrected causing the truck to swing around the other way. The rear quarter panel and bumper smashed into Naomi's Subaru, slid along the side, and crushed the steel as if it were made of tin foil. The camper wobbled, slid, but stayed upright.

The passenger side windows of the Subaru burst. Naomi ricocheted from right to left. She collided with the driver's side door, moaned, and blacked out again. Chris thought she would vacate her body once more from the trauma, but he didn't see her spirit leave. He jumped to his feet. The flash of Todd's sneering face as he rumbled by didn't last more than half a second. The truck already unstable after the collision, and with a reckless driver behind the wheel, hit the end of the driveway, took the turn onto the road, and rolled. Chris flinched as a horrific crunch of steel echoed down the street through the morning air. The truck landed on its roof, tires spinning. The scream of approaching sirens told Chris help would soon be there.

With the windows shattered, he reached inside and unlocked the doors. Chris slipped off the medicine bag he wore around his neck and placed the leather cord over Naomi's head to keep her spirit within her body.

"Naomi, you must stay inside your body. The elements of earth, air, water, and fire now protect you. The four directions and the ancestors of my people protect you. Do not vacate this form. Stay and be healed. Be whole."

The way the impact tossed Naomi around inside the car, he guessed she suffered whiplash. Paramedics would be there in a few more seconds. They could stabilize her neck with a cervical collar. Until then, Chris squatted down next to her, channeling healing energy and praying for her body and spirit.

"Good thing I shoved you out of the way. You might be knocked out like she is," Talks to the Wind said from behind him.

Chris wanted to point out that if he had held his ground, Naomi and her car would have been protected. He bit back the cutting remarks. "How about some help?"

"Not my area of expertise."

"Anyone can channel Great Spirit's universal energy and put it to use," Chris said trying his hardest to remain levelheaded.

"You're doing fine on your own."

Chris wondered again, for at least the tenth time that morning, why Talks to the Wind was his guide.

"You have a knack for finding good looking women with extraordinary gifts. If I were in your moccasins, I would gift her father a hundred of my best horses. You know," Talks to the Wind said thoughtfully, "the other woman was never right for you, but this one has potential."

"You can leave now if you're going to stand there and do nothing," Chris told Talks to the Wind. He was certain his guide was referring to Juliana. Talks to the Wind was right; Juliana was definitely not meant to be Chris's girlfriend. Juliana and Nathaniel were together, and Chris could not imagine anything in this world — or the next — that would tear them apart. He'd made peace with her decision to date the fallen angel. They were good for one another.

"Whatever you say," Talks to the Wind said. "I can't handle all this pressure in the air. It's dragging on me." He gestured toward the destruction that used to be Jack's Corner Pocket and left. Chris wasn't sad to see him go.

A host of shrieking sirens raced toward them. Two sheriffs, an ambulance, and a firetruck tore down the street and parked.

Naomi whimpered, and her eyes opened. Before Chris could tell her to hold still, she murmured, "Wakey, wakey, eggs and bakey."

He didn't know where she came up with the nonsensical babble. He was starting to get used to it, and even anticipated when she might say something that made him cringe and wonder at the same time.

"We need help over here!" He waved his arm in the air to get their attention. The paramedics rushed over with their gear, and Chris reported what little he knew about Naomi Hutson.

Chapter Five

CHRIS ARRIVED at the construction site well before sunrise. Autumn was kind to the mountains this year, providing warm, dry days, but the nights plummeted to near freezing temperatures. He climbed out of the truck and zipped up his insulated vest. If his ceremony failed this morning, at least he'd be warm in his layers of vest, T-shirt, and flannel. Not that he expected to fail, but he never expected a vortex to spiral out of the Earth in the middle of town either. Times were changing. The Earth was changing. His guides informed him on more than one occasion that the changes they witnessed since the turn of the century were occurring faster than they had ever seen. He always paid close attention to the messages from Spirit and tried to use the information wisely. Chris gathered his medicine bundle and approached the empty lot and energy vortex with his supernatural shields in place. He wouldn't be caught off guard this time.

The ground near the center of the vortex appeared to have risen a few feet as if being shoved upward from beneath. The skid loader sat at a hazardous angle near the trench where Marlin worked the morning before. A slew of ghosts hovered around the lot like unearthly guards. Chris's eyes burned from lack of sleep and his body dragged as heavy as his eyelids. Regardless of the detrimental sleep loss, his mind remained in overdrive.

Yesterday passed in a whirl of activity. After the excitement at Jack's Corner Pocket, he rode with Naomi to the hospital, stayed by her side through the check-in process, and then visited the police station. By the time he was finished filing the police report, he had needed to find something to eat. He drove to his father's house to consult with him on the unusual case.

Sherman White Wolf Abeyta shared food with his son and told stories through the night. Chris gained much-needed insight regarding the ghost world and energy shifts. In the early hours of the morning, he asked his father to come to town with him, but the elder shook his head and told his son he didn't feel like it.

Chris had his own interpretation of his father's refusal. Sherman once told him that he should develop his own methods and medicines for working with Spirit — without outside influence. Chris believed his father shared those words because he knew his son better than anyone else did. The elder understood that Chris worked best alone.

With Todd and Marlin's hasty departure the morning before, the gate hung open and no one had returned to lock it. Chris walked unhindered onto the lot. He concentrated on all that needed to be done. He couldn't relax or rest until the vortex was stable and the spirits, who arrived with the increase of Earth energy, passed to the spirit world.

Someone tapped him on the shoulder, and he steeled his resolve before responding.

"I am not here. Pretend you do not see me."

"Fat chance," the hefty male spirit said. He stood with fists resting against pudgy hips.

"Excuse me." Chris stepped to the side to make his way around the rotund man and immediately received a poke in the chest.

"I expect you're not walking away without assistance, so why don't you let me help you?"

The ghost grabbed the edge of Chris's vest near the shoulder — an unfortunate move.

Chris expected a protest from the ghosts at the construction site. He didn't know how powerful and belligerent they would be after figuratively sucking off the tit of Mother Nature for the past twenty-four hours. The negative vortex at Jack's attracted the worst of the worst, regarding damaged souls, but the ones on Hermosa Ave. were of a different ilk. These ghosts chose to remain in spirit form for their own reasons, but not because they were fiendish or banished. The ghosts on Hermosa Ave. were the type to mourn the loss of a loved one or brood in a battlefield for all eternity — not create chaos and evil like the ghosts flocking to the pool hall. These lost spirits were mostly harmless, that is until something set them off. Such as feeding them a pure stream of Earth energy and then trying to take it away.

A crowd gathered around him and the bully. He watched their second line of defense move into place in an attempt to surround the core of the vortex. Chris didn't want a fight, and he certainly didn't want to make an example of this man, but with the physical contact, it couldn't be avoided.

Before the stout man had a chance to blink, let alone cast Chris off the property, the shaman concentrated the life force energy running through him into his palms. He slapped his hands over the man's ears and squeezed. The ghost yowled as Chris turned him into a shriveled specter, wretched, withered and unrecognizable. The group of spirits took a collective step back, but Chris felt them rallying almost instantly for another go at him. It wouldn't take long for an impudent spirit to try again. Feeding off the vortex was like no other fountain of youth on the planet. If he had to guess, they wouldn't give up, and he was outnumbered fifty-to-one.

"I call upon the warriors. I call to my elders. Assist me as I am your humble brother. I ask for your help!"

Chris's voice carried all the way to the spirit world. He held what was left of the insolent spirit in one fist and knelt to open the flap on his bearskin medicine bundle. He removed a stone bottle and pulled the cork out with his teeth. He poured the mixture of corn pollen, tobacco, and crushed copal over the diminutive specter. The ghost dissolved and turned to ashes, scattering over the dirt like dust. The wayward ghost would not return to the spirit world and would forever be less than even what the worms fed on.

He sprinkled the medicinal mixture over his open palms to cleanse them of any etheric residue. Satisfied with the results, he stuffed the cork in the bottle and glanced up. Chris's call for help had been answered.

The desire to step back and observe the battle from a spectator's point of view ached in his nostalgic bones. Dozens of warriors from the past arrived along with many medicine men. They attacked the rebellious horde of ghosts in full regalia — and every brave looked as if he thirsted for battle. Only in his mind and imagination had he ever conjured a sight like the one before him. Painted warriors, brandishing their weapons captured and took down one lost spirit after another. Valor and fearlessness surged through his chest and drove him forward. Chris could not stand aside and watch. He pounced on the nearest ghost, wrapped an arm around his neck, and squeezed. The battle cry whooped out of him, devastating and victorious.

The fight didn't last long. By the time Chris sent his ghost to the spirit world, each of his otherworldly helpers had captured a lost soul and dragged them off to a higher dimension where souls renew and rest in peace. The warriors did not return. His four main spirit guides came back to the lot, smiling, and congratulating each other on a successful battle. The four were a wise group of ancient medicine men who often stood by Chris's side when he performed ceremonies.

"The young one is always bringing us much excitement," Yellow Hawk said.

"He is the new generation. His medicine is strong," Two Suns remarked.

Chris waited patiently for his guides to finish talking before moving on to the real reason they were there.

"That was the largest group of unsettled souls I have ever seen," Black Horns said.

"An impressive group," Bill agreed. "Quite lively for the displaced. How is it you have gathered a large number of them together, Chris?"

"It was not my doing," he said. "Take a look over there. Do you not feel it in the air and below your moccasins?" he asked Bill.

Bill would be considered the most modern of his four medicine men guides. And by modern, he estimated Bill's last incarnation was about one hundred and fifty years ago, give or take a couple of decades. The medicine man preferred to be called Bill and never gave anyone a more traditional name. Bill's broad face matched his broad chest. He had a wide flat nose above a mouth that was perpetually turned down. As he looked around the construction site, his lips compressed into an even deeper frown.

"An anomaly. Is that what you would call it?" Bill asked.

"That's a word for it," Chris said. "An energy vortex made by unearthing and rerouting the sacred waters. With your guidance, we will help our Great Mother this morning so she may heal. The vortex will remain, but it will not be wide open."

"You helped many suffering souls cross over this day. Great Spirit smiles on you. It is a mighty deed," Black Horns said solemnly.

Black Horn's acknowledgment received agreeable nods from the others.

Chris said, "I have done little. The warriors fought bravely. I do what I can, but it is nothing."

Their eyes crinkled and softened toward Chris. Remaining humble was a path they all aspired to stay on.

The five medicine men moved closer to the open trench and surveyed the damages and the haphazard repairs started by Marlin and Todd. Surprisingly, Todd or

Marlin managed to fix the broken pipeline before being scared off by the ghosts. The repair tamped down some of the energy flowing from the vortex and eased the external pressure on his spirit guides. Chris made a vital adjustment to an overflow valve by shutting off the flow of water completely so none of the hot spring water ran into the tributary stream. Keeping the two sources of water separated brought the land back to the way it was supposed to be, and harmony was restored. Chris climbed into the skid steer, and moved a small mountain of dirt, covering up the final section of open trench. Todd made a horrible mistake when they hit the piped hot spring. If he bothered to check the building plans, he could have avoided the disaster. Instead, he and Marlin learned the hard way. Chris didn't want anyone else to make the same mistake. He spent the next hour moving boulders from the creek bank and built a stone barricade over the vortex. When he could do no more, he parked the skid steer and retrieved his medicine bundle.

Each of the medicine men smoked from Chris's ceremonial pipe and said a prayer. Two Suns addressed the four directions. Yellow Hawk prayed to the gods above and below. Bill danced and sang a song to bring everlasting harmony. Black Horns created an impenetrable circle of protection, and Chris sealed the ceremony with a prayer and his sacred corn pollen, tobacco, and sage.

With the vortex hampered, the Earth energy in and around the empty lot settled to a reasonable level, and Chris began decompressing. His guides returned to the spirit world as he packed up his medicine bundle.

The sun rose and morning commuters could be heard driving down the main avenue through town. Chris sat in the cab of his truck and forced himself to stay awake. He had one final thing to take care of before he could go to sleep — the meeting with the city planner, the building department, Officer Howe, and the owner of the property, Mr. Schlitz, a.k.a. Todd's father and a known land developer.

The dread of the upcoming meeting — with actual living people — weighed heavy on his mind. The anxiety it created was a hundred times worse than any battle with parasitic energy-sucking ghosts. Chris drank some of the medicinal tea his father handed him hours earlier. The tea didn't quite provide the kick in the ass he needed for dealing with people — who would be arriving any second now — but it was all he had.

To his minor relief, Officer Howe arrived first. The others showed up minutes later. Chris drug himself from the truck and spent the next thirty minutes explaining and describing something most people thought of as intangible or make believe. Officer Howe believed in Chris, and his work as a shaman and ghost hunter, and affirmed Chris's statements and backed him up where he could.

Since Todd botched the excavating job from the very beginning, there wasn't much or any argument from his father, Mr. Schlitz. That is until Chris pointed out the environmental concerns for the underground hot spring. The city planner jumped in and put an immediate halt to the project until an environmental impact study could be conducted on the empty lot and the adjoining tributary stream. Then Officer Howe asked the building inspector why the lot appeared to be heaved upward in the center and pointed out how the empty building next door looked affected by this unusual shift in the ground. The inspector deemed more inspections must be made on the entire block before any further construction. Mr. Schlitz promptly went ballistic. Chris felt his job was complete and stepped away from the others.

Somehow, he drove himself home, even though he didn't remember doing so. A vague recollection of Talks to the Wind helping him out of the truck and up to his front door teased his memory. Would his guide actually drive the truck for him? He didn't know and didn't care. The only thing that held any importance was a mattress to stretch out on and the soft cushion of a pillow beneath his head.

Chapter Six

"THESE WILL KEEP you from exiting your body." Chris held up two strings of multi-colored beads.

"Do I wear them? Eat them? What am I looking at?" Naomi asked, squinting up at him.

Chris stepped closer to the hospital bed and handed over the bracelets.

Naomi inspected the beads and then hid the bracelets underneath the sheet. She brought her knees up as she fidgeted beneath the covers. Uncomfortable, he waited for her to finish. He thought he would see the talisman bracelets on her wrists when she stopped fiddling with them. He should know better than to assume anything involving Naomi.

"What did you do? They are for your protection. I worked hard to ensure the stone beads, and the charms will keep your spirit secure within your body. If you decide to astral travel in the future, you will need to take them off."

"I can feel your magic infused in them."

"It is not magic," he clarified.

"Whatever you want to call it," she said dismissively, then smiled. "I can feel the power. And they're on my ankles."

The pleased expression on her face caused him to hesitate. He intended for the charms to be worn around the wrists. Intention is a major factor in the creation and usage of his medicines. *Would it make a difference?*

While he thought about it, she asked, "What's with the sour face, mate?"

"Why did you put them on your ankles instead of your wrists?"

"They looked like anklets. They're somewhat long. Besides, I assumed they have to stay on all the time — considering my issues with astral projection. If they're on my ankles, I won't think twice about them."

"Very well," he said, satisfied with her answer. "I don't care to be called 'mate.'"

"How about Bucko?"

"Not working for me either."

"Silly-Billy?"

"Absolutely not."

"Wet blanket."

He didn't know if she still searched for an acceptable pet name or if she was calling him a "wet blanket." Probably the latter. Given the opportunity, Chris could dampen just about anyone's good mood.

"That one at least fits the bill."

A tiny smirk hid behind her full lips. Naomi lifted Chris's medicine pouch from around her neck. "I guess I don't need this anymore."

He reached for his medicine bag and put it back on where it belonged. He tucked the pouch beneath his shirt noticing the warmth of her skin on the leather. "Ready to get out of here?"

He returned to the hospital for more reasons than bringing Naomi the protective charm bracelets. Chris wanted to give her a ride and make her an offer.

She stared into her lap. "I don't have anywhere to go. My car is totaled, and I don't want to go back to the parking lot at work."

"Jack's Corner Pocket is no longer a problem. I took care of the vortices."

"Already? How?"

"I had to seal and control the vortex over on Hermosa. Once I accomplished that, the negative repercussions balanced themselves out. I went back to Jack's to make sure. I had some work to do. All is relatively normal now."

"Except for the demolished building," she added.

"Yes. Except that. Your boss told me this is the greatest thing that has ever happened to him."

"What?" Naomi asked, confused.

"Jack told me he is very well insured. Only the back of the building was destroyed, and the pool tables were all spared. They are saying the cause is an unknown structural failure."

"That sounds a lot like my diagnosis. I guess western medicine hasn't quite figured out astral projection and spiritual distress. The doctors have no idea how my brain works."

"They wouldn't know. Western medicine is very narrow thinking. It is one reason I stay in business. They are good at looking after muscles and bones. How is your neck?" He noticed she was not wearing a neck brace.

"It's a little sore but fine. I'll take it easy until I feel better." Uncertainty shadowed her face and Naomi glanced away. Chris watched her aura shift, financial concerns mingling with instability in the energetic field around her body.

"Your camper trailer is no longer parked at the billiard hall."

Her eyes widened in alarm. "Where's my house? Was it impounded?" Her fingers ran over her scalp, and she gripped two handfuls of hair and squeezed.

"I towed your camper to my house. I didn't want anyone to steal it or have it taken away with your car."

"You what? Really?"

"If you want, you can camp next to my cabin until your car is repaired or replaced."

"Are you kidding me right now, Mr. Medicine Man?"

"I am not kidding."

"Oh my God. Yes!"

"It is settled then."

"No, it isn't. I want to thank you. For everything. How about I make you dinner? In my camper. Tonight. Are you busy later?"

Chris wanted to help Naomi out. He didn't expect any form of payment. Letting her park the camper in his yard had been Talks to the Wind's idea. Naomi lost her car and her job in a matter of minutes. He was only doing what any decent person would do.

"You helped by making me aware of the vortices in town. The whole town owes you. I do not need anything from you in return. There's a wooded lot and plenty of space at my place. If you haven't figured it out, I am not a very social person. Dinner is not necessary."

"Okay, first of all, duh. You are one of the most awkward people I have ever met, and second, I sort of like that about you. Third, I'm going to cook something tonight. I don't know what, but you're coming over to eat with me so I can thank you."

Chris lowered his gaze, breaking eye contact with Naomi as he considered the multiple repercussions of having dinner with this woman. He glanced back up and saw a hint of expectancy and a touch of uncertainty in her beguiling liquid brown eyes as she waited for his response.

"What time?" he asked.

* * *

"I don't cook," she confessed.

Naomi stood by the miniature sink in her ridiculously tiny camper smiling at Chris. He stood just outside the door, peering in and making no move to enter.

"But I can order food to be delivered like a ninja."

"You don't cook," he reiterated.

"I can… I just don't. I mean, look at my kitchen. It's sort of small."

Chris coughed.

"Your face would suggest you're wondering why I asked you over for dinner?"

Chris ran a knuckle down the bridge of his nose. "You ordered take-out?"

Naomi laughed as she reached for a covered bowl on the counter. "Nope. I thought about it, but I didn't — this time."

The way she said "this time" hopefully implied there would be another dinner together in the future. Naomi wanted the chance to get to know Chris Abeyta better. He intrigued her, and that rarely happened. He gave off such mixed signals — something else that sparked her curiosity.

"Come on in, silly. It's ready and waiting."

Naomi placed the bowl on her converted bed/dining table, peeled the plastic lid off and spun around to grab the champagne. She hadn't heard Chris move and had no idea he stood right behind her.

Startled enough to make her heart skip, she jumped, placed her hands against his chest to stop herself from running into him and yelped. This elicited an eyebrow raise from Chris as he looked down at her hands and then into her eyes.

"Your house is even smaller than mine."

"It has everything I need." She didn't lower her hands. Chris may not be as large a guy as she was used to dating, but there was nothing soft about him. She felt the dense muscles of his chest through his vest and shirt. And he was taller than she remembered. Being out of body did strange things to one's perspective.

She made to move around him in the tiny square footage, and Chris went the same direction, they veered the other way, simultaneously correcting and ended up doing an awkward dance in the center of her travel trailer. Both stopped moving, her smiling, Chris frowning.

"Our first dance?"

"There's no music," he said.

They shimmied around each other, and Naomi grabbed the split of champagne from her mini fridge. "I can fix that."

Chris sat at the table as she set the champagne down, then turned to the shelf that held her MP3 player and docking station. Her crystal prayer grid glowed softly, working its magic. After the accident, her grid had been a jumbled pile of stones, copper wire, and scraps of paper. Rebuilding turned out to be a good thing. Starting over from scratch felt cleansing and that made her happy. Naomi chose her coffee shop playlist, a mix of acoustic rock, jazz, bluegrass, and other songs that didn't require head banging, mosh pits, or anything else inappropriate for an intimate dinner.

Before sitting down with Chris at the table, she did something she hardly ever showed anyone. She thought Chris would accept her skills without question, or fear. Naomi picked up the small box of matches from the table and lit one. She held the flame in front of her, closed her eyes, and then lightly blew the flame toward the table. The match extinguished, but the tiny orange and yellow flame rolled like a ball through the air toward the food. The fire darted beneath the pot, lighting the chafing fuel with a whoosh of blue flame, then soared over and landed in Naomi's green pillar candle, lighting the wick. She waved a hand at the curtains surrounding the table, and they pulled aside letting in the evening light.

Chris remained motionless as she worked her minor magic, but a smile sat on his lips when she was done. She slid into the seat opposite him.

"Now it's ready. Dive in. Oh, wait. One last thing." She concentrated on the small bottle of champagne, visualizing the bubbles and the air inside pushing upward and out of the bottle. The cork shot out, hit the ceiling, and ricocheted across the trailer. "I forgot to open that."

"You are harmonious with the air."

She beamed. She knew he'd understand. "Just as you are with the spirit world."

"In a way."

She winked at him, and they picked up their forks.

"This is how you don't cook." Chris gestured to the fondue pot and the plates of cut up vegetables, meat, and bread.

"This isn't cooking. This is simple."

"It's more cooking than I generally do."

"But you're a dude. Most men I know don't really cook. They just heat stuff up. Which is sort of what we're doing now."

He didn't agree or disagree but dipped another chunk of French bread into the melted cheese.

After he had finished chewing, he said, "And the champagne is better than I thought it would be. It complements the fondue."

"I'm glad you like it. I've been saving it until I found a vortex. I always celebrate when I find a new one."

"I'm sorry you were not there to see when I closed it."

"Don't apologize. I feel it in the air and under the ground. It's not as strong as the first morning, but it still exists."

Chris nodded as he tried a piece of beef in the cheese sauce. "It was like capping a well. The vortex is a powerful one. It needed to be restricted. I don't have to explain it all. You saw what happened when it was fully open."

She watched him carefully and felt the intention in his words. "It's nice to talk about it with someone who understands. I'm going to guess you don't have someone to talk with about your work very often?" She made it a question.

Chris delayed answering. She wondered if she inadvertently crossed a line with him. Like most witches she knew, she was highly sensitive to other people and their behavior and attitudes. Empathy had its rewards, but also its challenges.

He leaned against the backrest, forearms resting on the table. "Most days speaking to anyone is a horrible effort. I would skip it altogether if I could get away with it. Right now, I don't mind talking to you about the case. I'm not sure what to make of the connection between us. This is new for me."

Naomi considered this pronouncement for a second. "I guess with the right company, anything can happen," she said cheerily and dipped an apple slice in the cheese.

"Or, I've been possessed."

"Oh, but Mr. Shaman, you're way too powerful to be influenced by some puny little evil spirit."

"Anything can happen," he said flatly, but a half smile teased the side of his mouth as he mimicked her words.

They dipped and twirled cheese on the ends of their fondue forks for a few minutes, then Chris said, "There are many new birds in my yard today."

As if on cue, a robin sang out as if to rule the neighborhood. The birdsong filled the camper, overriding the music playing through the speakers.

"They follow me," she admitted.

"I like it. They sound happy that you are here. I think the bird population has tripled."

"I'm happy to be here too," she said. If that wasn't a blunt hint she was interested, she didn't know what was.

"Do you hear them at five o'clock in the morning?"

"I don't. I sleep like a rock… a rock beneath a rock. Not much gets through when my eyes are closed."

"Good to know," he said. "You were the same way out of body."

"That doesn't surprise me." Naomi was subtly making up her mind about Chris and how far she would go with him. Her gut knew she would go all the way if he hinted any attraction to her. She was curious, but so much more than that. Her nerve endings sizzled when she was near him, and the butterflies were on crack. It had been a long time since there had been butterflies and she couldn't ignore it. And that kiss. He kissed as if he was interested.

"Do you want to eat dessert outside? Listen to the birds while we eat chocolate?"

Chris's gaze lowered to the table where no chocolate was in sight. Was this mixed signals again, or was she trying too hard to figure him out?

"Sure," he said.

She rose from the table and grabbed the tray of fruit and cake. She turned to hand it over to Chris. Once again, he stood behind her without her hearing him move. It was unnerving. Then it dawned on her that when she astral traveled she most likely did the same thing to him. Although Chris, of all people, would be used to being around others who never made any physical sound... since they didn't exist in the third dimension. "Can you carry this for me?"

He took the dessert tray, and she picked up the small covered pot from the stove. Chris led her through the gate and around the side of the cabin to his patio where he placed the tray on the table.

"Will you start the fire? I'd like to see you practice your craft again." He nodded toward the stone fire pit built into the patio. Kindling wood sat in the center waiting to be lit.

A crisp nip in the autumn evening gave her baby goose bumps — not full-fledged goose bumps but smaller ones. A fire would be perfect to lift the chill.

Naomi placed the chocolate fondue pot on the table and turned her attention to the fire ring. She wanted to cast an illusion this time and considered how to go about it. With Chris watching, a tiny amount of expectancy warmed the center of her chest. She listened to the robin belting out his evening song and heard the fluttering wings of a junco as it darted across the patio. She glanced skyward for a moment, thinking, and noticed the first star of the night. Then she had it.

Naomi murmured under her breath. "Star light, star night. Cast away all that is bright. Let yourself be the only one, and share with me your fire until I say you're done." A soft wind brought the smells of fall, dry earth, and leaf mulch. Dead grasses rustled as the illusion of midnight fell over them like a black veil. The single star Naomi had been watching fell from the heavens in an arc of blue flame. The star came to rest mere inches in front of her nose. Naomi snapped her fingers and pointed to the fire pit. The star shot over to the stone ring and dove beneath the splintered kindling wood. A shower of neon blue and white sparks danced around the twigs and branches until a small flame ignited. The orange and yellow fire lifted the enchantment, and the backyard came into focus. Pleased with her creativity and spontaneity on demand, she played it cool by walking over to the pot of warm chocolate sauce and removing the lid.

"What's your favorite thing to dip in chocolate?" She uncovered the tray and picked up a strawberry.

Chris's gaze held steady on the growing flames. "Great Spirit gave us the stars. The Sacred Mother gives us life. It is rare to find someone blessed with many gifts from both Creator and his counterpart." His eyebrows rose and fell as if contemplating and accepting Naomi's talents in one subtle yet expressive gesture. His eyes shifted to her face. If she weren't mistaken, his appreciation of her magic passed like an invisible current from him to her, stroking her ego without using any further words. She smiled as she dipped the berry in the chocolate.

He continued. "I don't know what I like to dip. I've never eaten chocolate fondue before."

She caught herself before her jaw dropped. It never occurred to her that someone could go through life without having eaten chocolate dipped strawberries… or apples, pound cake, and pretzels. *Who was this guy?* She needed to correct this depravity. "Then you have to try everything."

He sat down next to her at the table and Naomi winked as she handed him a strawberry covered in silky smooth dark chocolate.

"Pretzels and blueberries," Chris said after trying one of each item on the tray. "And you like all of it."

"I do." She grinned and reached for the last marshmallow.

"This is more chocolate than I have ever eaten in one sitting. Excuse me one minute." Chris rose from the table and went inside through the back door of the cabin.

Naomi wondered if he went inside to be sick. Wouldn't that be a great story to tell later? The title could be, Naomi's Dates Gone Tragically Awry. But Chris didn't say anything about being ill. He returned twice. Once carrying two large glasses of water, and the second time holding a bottle of wine and two wine glasses.

"The water helps wash down all the sugar," he explained after drinking his entire glass. He placed a hand on the cobalt blue wine bottle. "Would you like to share this with me? I don't normally drink wine, but a client gave it to me. Since you like champagne, I thought you might like this as well."

Naomi read the label. "I'm down for a little Moscato d'Asti. Maybe it will be my new favorite wine to go with the cake and blueberries. They are my two favorites today."

Chris poked the corkscrew from his pocketknife into the top of the bottle and twisted. He pulled the cork out with the anticipated 'pop' of released air and filled two glasses. He moved his chair closer to the fire and Naomi did the same.

As Chris added a log to the fire, he asked, "Does your favorite food change often?"

"Of course. It's a woman's prerogative to change her mind."

"Is that so?"

She was getting used to his deadpan looks. And more than that, used to the subtle shifts of his almost unreadable expressions. "Absolutely," she flirted.

"That's frightening."

"It's good for a man to be a little scared by a woman." She sipped her wine and watched him over the rim of the glass.

"I think you just touched the edge of a little-known wisdom."

Naomi didn't have a chance to reply, even though the quip sat on the tip of her tongue. For an entirely different reason, Chris was not the only one who was scared now. Naomi let out a piercing yelp as a shadow appeared behind Chris — and spoke.

"My favorite brother is having a ceremonial fire and did not invite me. What did I do to shame you? Where are the medicine men?"

The ghost stepped into the light and Naomi saw it was Talks to the Wind. Only she saw him from Chris's lap. Her arms were around his neck, and she buried her face against his chest. She glanced up to see Chris looking surprised if not shocked to find her seated on top of him.

She honestly didn't remember moving. Naomi did a double take to make sure she had not jumped out of her body. Then she remembered the anklets, and how they kept her from astral projecting. Apparently, they worked great.

"You are mistaken. I have no ceremonial fire tonight."

With arms crossed in front of his chest, Talks to the Wind looked them over. His gaze shifted to the table, the leftover food, and the bottle of wine. A slow smile spread across his wide mouth.

"You're having a night with your new woman. The guides and I like this one. I am glad she has not run off to find someone not as ugly as you."

Naomi wanted to defend Chris's looks. He wasn't ugly at all. In her opinion, he was extremely good looking. That is, if imploring sexy eyes above cut cheekbones, a strong jaw, a lean torso, and sinewy sculpted muscles meant a man was good looking. It certainly did to Naomi. He was hot. Then she realized the insults were part of the banter.

"Did you need something? Or are you here to generally annoy and disturb my night off?"

"Annoy? What is this annoy? I am unfamiliar with your English words."

Naomi knew he had a perfectly fine grasp on the English language and continued to taunt Chris.

"Not now, Talks to the Wind. I'm off duty." Chris reached down and set his wineglass on the patio. He was careful not to tip Naomi off his lap. She saw her own wineglass near the chair leg and could not for the life of her remember placing it there.

Talks to the Wind's grin spread into a wide smile. The gap between his front teeth flashed before he disappeared back from wherever he had come from. She shivered and ducked her head again. Goddess help her. She was never going to get used to spirits and ghosts.

This could become a real issue considering she wanted to date a ghost hunting shaman.

"I almost forgot. I have interesting information for Fish Face. It can wait until you're back on duty."

She heard Talks to the Wind's voice as if he sat next to them, even though he was no longer visible. Her hypersensitive nature, combined with the fear, sent a shiver colder than dry ice cascading through her bloodstream. Naomi shuddered and promptly passed out.

"You can come back now," Chris said over her. He gently nudged her cheek as he spoke. "Talks to the Wind will not be back tonight. Naomi, wake up. His visit is not that upsetting."

His baritone timbre lulled, enticed, and pulled at her. She drifted back to consciousness and opened her eyes. She breathed deep until her heartbeat returned to normal. Naomi stared up into the depths Chris's nearly black eyes and glimpsed a soft side to the shaman. She saw a man with bottomless empathy and a soul so ancient that time seemed to disappear.

Naomi ran her hand up his chest until she cupped the back of his neck. She sat up and guided him to meet her halfway. He closed the gap between them and their lips met, tentative in the beginning, but a rush of pleasure and need passed between them like lightning.

It was spontaneous and thrilling. She hadn't wanted to be with anyone since before she packed up her car and camper and left home in search of vortices, which had been over six months ago. Oh yeah, Naomi was ready to fool around. She was more than ready, and Chris seemed of a similar mind. They rose from the patio chair, kissing as they stumbled toward the door to the cabin. The screen door swung open, and Chris held her against the doorjamb kissing her properly before moving through the sunroom to the hallway. Her back to the wall, and his leg pressed between her thighs, Chris nibbled her earlobe and asked, "What are we doing?"

"Getting to know each other better." She was certainly getting better acquainted with the muscles beneath his shirt.

"This is okay with you?" he asked as his mouth traveled to the small divot above her collarbone.

"Oh, definitely."

A low masculine groan rumbled out of his throat. Chris whisked her away from the wall, pivoted, and guided her through the nearest doorway. Naomi found herself kissing Chris on the bed. She didn't stop there, and neither did he.

Chapter Seven

"I COULD NEVER be in a relationship with a smoker."

Naomi took a drag off the clove cigarette. She exhaled, blowing the smoke away from Chris. "Geez, judgmental much?"

"Against poisoning myself? Yes, I am."

"So you think you're being exposed to second-hand smoke and the chemicals in my cigarette are poisoning you?" She stubbed out the poison in question.

"Correct."

"But you admit to using tobacco on a fairly regular basis with your ceremonies." She tipped her head to the side and eyed him on an angle. "Let me guess. That's entirely different."

"It is."

"Well, what if I told you smoking is medicinal? It soothes my anxiety and helps me focus."

Chris's steady gaze remained cautious, and he tried to hide the humor he always seemed to feel when he spoke with her. She wasn't lying — *exactly*. Naomi's beguiling deceptions were more in line with manipulating the truth to suit one's needs. Her cunning and crafty womanly ways enticed him as much as terrified. Part of him knew he should run, forget about her, and part of him wanted to take her straight to his bed. It was a precarious conundrum he'd never found himself in before. "Medicine and vice are two different things."

"Touché, Mr. Abeyta, touché." Naomi dug into her shoulder bag and took out a piece of candy. The wrapper crinkled and then she popped the candy into her mouth. Sweet green apple scented the air. "Oh, and by the way, I quit. I'm no longer a smoker," she said around the candy.

Chris snorted. He actually snorted at her declaration. "You quit right now?"

"I did. You gave up your solitude to let me camp here, and I gave up cigarettes."

"I will believe it when I see it." Chris rose from the patio chair and looked out over the yard. The birds were going crazy — again. Anytime Naomi stepped outside they sang, chirped, and fluttered from branch to branch. He began imagining he lived in a bird sanctuary.

Chris spent the entire day focused on a new case, and he was in a quiet mood. He had not talked to her since the day before, even though she lived thirty feet from his front door.

"Have you ever had a major head injury?" she asked.

He cast a barbed stare her direction and waited for her to get to the point. Innocent, she was not. He knew Naomi was having fun at his expense.

"If I have, I don't have a recollection of it."

She laughed and the sound mingled with the birds. "Good answer. So, I'll say that you had a brain injury, and that would explain a lot about you."

"You're so kind," he said with a hint of bitterness that wasn't really bitter at all. She was probably correct in her assessment.

"I don't have to be kind. You just told me you would never date a smoker."

"And you told me you no longer are one."

"Well, well, boyo, does that mean we are officially dating? I mean I have seen you naked and all. And I sort of approve if you wanted to take this… whatever this is." She waved a slender hand in the air gesturing from him to her. "To the next level."

"You have been staying the night in my house. I was under the impression we had moved to the next level." *Great Spirit help him. He would never understand the inner workings of the female mind.*

"You just said you would never be in a relationship with someone who smoked."

Naomi seemed confused.

He revised. "I have been trying to decide if you are a smoker. I have only seen you with clove cigarettes three times since we met six weeks ago."

"Because I smoke occasionally, just like you do."

"It is not like I do. I use tobacco for ceremonial purposes."

"Haven't we circled this block before?"

Chris eyed her from his peripheral vision. Her aura would suggest she was completely at ease. His aura, on the other hand, roiled in a colorful mess of emotions. No woman had ever bewildered him quite this much. One part of him could not take the turmoil and another part of him wanted more. It was all very confusing. The contentment he experienced when he woke up next to her in the morning felt solid, real, and lodged in his psyche. But she smoked. That turned him off as much as if she were addicted to gambling or alcohol.

"You're right. We have. We are moving on to a new subject," he said.

"Canoodling? We both like that subject."

"No. I mean yes, no. Later. Maybe." Flustered, he gave her a quizzical glance and frowned. "Where do you come up with these words?"

"Not everyone is as stiff and formal as you are, Mr. Deadpan Medicine Man."

Chris ran a hand over his five o'clock shadow.

"So if we're not snogging, what's up?"

Thrown off course, Chris had to think for a second before remembering what he wanted to say. "Talks to the Wind told me about a vortex in the Four Corners region. He says it is largely unknown."

"When did he tell you this?"

"Early this morning when I worked outside."

"I've been meaning to thank you for asking him to not come inside when I'm here."

"It is nothing. Very few spirits, you being one of them, and only my guides can enter my cabin without permission. Talks to the Wind can knock on the door like any other guest."

"Still, it's thoughtful of you. Tell him I appreciate it."

"You can tell him. He will be back tomorrow. He wants to share his news with you. I told him you would not pass out again if he arrived in the form of a living person."

Naomi cocked a brow. "Let me guess. Talks to the Wind said, 'Why should I knock? I like scaring Fish Face.'"

Chris grinned. “You know him well already.”

“I’m not sure if that’s a good thing.” Naomi shifted her bag aside on the patio table and rose to her feet.

“Better to go with the flow when it comes to Talks to the Wind.”

“Go with the flow?” she mocked. “I think I’m starting to rub off on you.”

Chris scratched his head and didn’t remark on her observation. Instead, he returned to the subject of the vortex. “Will you try to find it?”

“A new power place? Yeah, absolutely. That’s why I’m out West. I want to find as many as I can.”

“When your car is finally fixed or before?” He didn’t want to think about her leaving. This realization equally surprised and worried him. Was he so attached to Naomi that the thought of her leaving town upset him?

Naomi stood in front of him and tipped her face up to his. She raised her hand and brushed her mass of curls away from her face. Her hair hung loosely today, instead of being held back with a headband or in braids. He liked it when she let it down. There was so much of it, like a black and sable mane around her stunning face.

“I don’t know when I’ll go. I never planned to stay in the mountains for the winter. The snow is already starting to stick to the ground. Camper trailers aren’t the warmest accommodations.”

He returned her gaze. Eye contact with Naomi was always extreme. She stared into him, and he wasn’t used to anyone seeing him naked.

“If I had a boyfriend, he might offer to go with me. If he had a truck, we could tow my trailer and camp together.”

The smile took him a moment, but before he let it show, he said, "That *would* be nice of your boyfriend. Do I know him? I would offer some advice on your nutritional habits or lack of them. Your fear of ghosts should be noted as well."

Naomi's lips tightened, and her eyes narrowed the slightest amount. He clearly saw the hot-tempered Korean blood she inherited from her mother. Getting a rise out of her could be so interesting. Her aura would shift from soft pastels that reached out toward him to sharp contrasting colors that poked and prodded at his etheric body.

She stood taller. "There is nothing wrong with what I like to eat."

It took a lot of concentration to keep the grin from escaping. "You think eating a bag of cheese popcorn and drinking a mimosa is a healthy dinner — or breakfast."

Her mouth popped open, and she did the "fish lips" thing. Chris hardened his jaw. Now he wanted to laugh aloud. Naomi huffed and started to walk away. Chris snagged her hand and reeled her in.

"I am joking with you, Fish Face."

"Did I ever tell you not to call me that, buddy-boy?"

"Did I ever tell you I do not like being called anything other than Chris?" He wrapped his arms around her waist and held her against him. She didn't pull away from the embrace.

"I'm sure you have, Mr. Sourpuss."

Chris's brows gathered as he considered her for a moment. She irked him. She didn't cook. She was the most loosely connected person to the physical realm he'd ever met. She was currently unemployed and lived wherever the winds blew. Her magic astounded him and her irrational fear of spirits and other entities charmed him. He couldn't get enough of her.

"I have an idea. Well, it wasn't my idea. Rumor has it that I am not as smart as the person who came up with it. This person believes I suffered a closed head injury at some point in my life."

Naomi suppressed a giggle. "I like this person. What did she say?"

"She thinks I should hook up my girlfriend's camper trailer to my truck and go search for an energy vortex together."

"Your girlfriend?" Naomi asked.

"That's right. What do you think about that?"

"I think it's an outstanding idea."

The smile he held back finally escaped. Expectation and anticipation flashed through her bewitching eyes as she tipped her full lips up to his. He nearly missed her cue. Being in a relationship would probably kill him, but for Naomi, he was willing to try. He leaned down and kissed her before missing his chance. She responded to him with equal desire. He wanted this, he realized. He wanted her. And he looked forward to whatever the future held in store for them.

Thank you for reading.

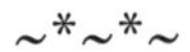

If you enjoyed reading *The Misplaced*, please help spread the word. The greatest compliment you could give is to write a review at your favorite online retailer, share with a book club, or recommend it to a friend.

Bonus Novella

THE CALL

An Angel Falls Novella

Ghost Hunting With Chris Abeyta

JODY A. KESSLER

Please visit:
www.JodyAKessler.com
Sign up for the newsletter

Edited by
Simon Oneill & Nancy Segovia

Cover Art & Design by
Laura Moyer

Chapter One

CHRIS ABEYTA BREATHED in the cool alpine air surrounding Tava Mountain. The majestic peak towered over him like a monolith to the Gods. All around him the San Juan Mountains were awakening and greeting the morning. The first day of fall had a crisp nip to the air but the sky was mostly clear with a positive outlook for warm weather.

Chris had chosen to rise before dawn and make the trek up to his favorite spot on the mountainside to greet the sun with a clear mind and to reset his intentions for the coming fall and winter. The spirit of the mountain now spoke to him with the characteristic beauty of the earth and sky and all that lay between.

His breaths came slow and even while listening to the breeze rustle the scrub oaks, whisper through the golden aspen leaves and blend with the chatter of the birds and squirrels. As the sprawling vista transformed from darkness to light he watched the rays of the sun strike the granite rock face above him and crawl down the mountain until he could feel its warmth upon his face.

His serene and peaceful moment was suddenly interrupted by the cell phone buzzing inside his vest pocket. Chris scowled and promptly ignored the call. As far as he was concerned, the importance of the despised electronic leash ranked lower than the mysterious sticky substance stuck to his boot heel. He suspected he'd picked up the manure while crossing the meadow on his way up to timberline but it was inconsequential. Shit on his shoe was a fact of life. It'd rub off soon enough. The phone inside his pocket, however, was a mistake he'd made by unconscious choice. If he'd remembered the blasted thing was with him, he would have left it in the truck, turned off.

He wondered why he even owned one as he let it go to voicemail. Business, his brain reminded him, and family—but mostly for business. If he wanted to continue paying his bills he had to operate his ghost hunting business like a professional. Much to his annoyance, his clients liked to be able to get a hold of him at their convenience, not his.

Switching gears, Chris tried to forget about the phone, and refocus his mind. When it didn't work, he rose from his perch on a boulder, chugged some water from his bottle, and set off, hiking back to his truck.

He descended the mountain, traversing over the sub-alpine terrain. As he passed through a dense section of coniferous forest the phone beeped letting him know he had a message waiting for him. Before he had a chance to turn off the phone, he saw the dead body lying in his path. He stared down at it, surprised. The dead raven had not been there on his way up. He would have seen it. Chris knew this was not to be ignored.

He glanced around the forest and up to the tree tops before touching it. Silence surrounded him and he turned up his extrasensory perception. The forest is not normally a quiet place, but it could be at times, like right now. He sensed nothing unusual other than the unnatural stillness and let his guard down a fraction of an inch. Aware that ravens often have mates, he paid extra attention to the trees for any black eyes on him or the deceased bird in front of his boots. Nothing watched him and he accepted the fact that Creator had placed the bird before him for a reason, even if he was currently unaware of the reason.

The raven on the trail appeared uninjured, healthy and whole. He carefully flipped it over to see its underside, but could make no diagnosis on how it had died. If Creator wanted him to have raven medicine this day, he would take it with great care and respect.

Chris removed a small pipe from his backpack and packed the bowl with a sacred smoking mixture of his own making. Squatting down, he lit the pipe and blew the smoke over the bird until his bowl was empty. He said prayers for the raven spirit's safe passage to the afterlife before picking it up. Feeling certain this raven's life was part of a higher purpose, he used his bone-handled knife and took the wings and feet. He placed everything in a canvas sack and set about burying the remains. With the head of the bird pointing west, Chris covered the body with dirt and placed stones on top of the grave in a circle with the four directions in the center. He sprinkled offerings of tobacco and corn pollen, and said one more prayer for the raven and another one of gratitude.

He gathered the canvas sack, his backpack, and checked to make sure his knife was secure on his belt. The unmistakable niggling of his heightened awareness and sensitivities toward the supernatural told him he would need the raven with him as a protector or as a possible messenger from the void. The voicemail alert sounded for a second time. As he hiked down the path toward his pickup, he reached inside his pocket with the intent of turning the annoying phone off like it should have been in the first place. Later, when he returned home, he would muster up enough mental fortitude to deal with whoever wanted him. He tickled the power button to wake it up but the screen stayed black. The phone was already off. He gave it a skeptical look, glanced down at the bag in his hand containing the remnants of the raven and dually noted the otherworldly synchronicities firing at him.

Chris glanced up at the overcast sky. Clouds the color of pale ashes had moved in without him realizing it. The sun, brilliant and optimistic only an hour or two earlier, was now veiled by clouds. He reached in all directions with his mental and intuitive senses. Nothing spoke to him on any level, physical or spiritual, other than the odd silence. He moved on and saw his truck parked at the base of the hill along the forest service road. He set his objective to pay extra heed to the workings of the universe around him until the current mysteries revealed themselves, or until the signs slowed down and stopped. A single raven called in the distance and Chris listened for an answer from a fellow raven. When no other corvid responded, he knew the raven was confirming his intentions.

Inside his truck he powered up his phone and checked for the message that Great Spirit had alerted him of. A possible new client wanted to speak to him about a job. She didn't give any details other than her phone number and how she had found him. The otherworldly signs were too strong to be disregarded, and as much as he wanted to ignore the message for a day or two, he returned her call before leaving the forest. *What happened to the good ol' days when you could be left alone in the woods?* Listening to the phone ring, he decided he needed to move away. Somewhere where cell towers and sat phones didn't exist. Moving to Mars appealed to him on every level. Then he remembered even the distant planet wasn't exempt from spying satellites and intrusive human beings.

He kept the call brief and to the point. After hanging up, he held the damned device out the window and thought about chucking it into the bushes. He pulled his hand back in knowing he'd be at the store next week for another phone. Instead, he turned it off and tossed it inside the center console.

Chapter Two

CHRIS PULLED UP in front of a red brick home with a tidy, drought-friendly xeriscaped front yard. The spruce-green front door was the only thing that made this nondescript home stand out among the average middle-class eighties neighborhood.

He double-checked the address number on the note he'd written and confirmed he was sitting in front of the right house. Mrs. Patricia Mancos received his number from a past client. His business seemed to be growing steadily and the referral was appreciated, but the phone message from Mrs. Mancos disturbed him on a deeper level. He wasn't quite sure why, except to say the woman's voice held a certain tone of distress and distrust that scurried over his flesh like furious ants. Chris didn't want to reject the case based on one message and a slightly disturbing short phone call with Mrs. Mancos. The consultation would give him the additional information needed to know if whether or not he would accept the job.

Mrs. Mancos answered the door with a weak smile and invited him in. She led him to the dining table and offered him a glass of tea or some coffee.

"No, thank you," he said as he pulled out a chair and sat down on the cracked vinyl seat.

The smell inside the house hit him with mixed information. It said that the occupants had eaten, or were going to eat something from a slow cooker, someone smoked cigarettes, and the old carpet and outdated furniture gave it an aura and odor from thirty years ago. The décor, state of wear and tear, and overall ambiance of the house should have felt normal and comfortable to him, but it didn't. Chris had simple tastes and average standards. Even though Mrs. Mancos's home fit the bill for his "typical" clientele, the place vibrated with an undercurrent that kept him wary.

She fidgeted by the counter, picked up a glass, filled it with iced tea and then joined him.

"As I mentioned on the phone, my brother and I would like to hire you to find our cousin, Katrina Caldwell."

"I am not a detective, Mrs. Mancos."

"But you are a ghost hunter," Mrs. Mancos said with certainty.

"That is true."

"And you can communicate with the dead? That is what I was told."

"In certain circumstances, I can. The departed must be cooperative for open communication. If your cousin is deceased and lost among us, I may be able to speak with her. If she departed and is with the ancestors, I will most likely not be able to find her. Letting spirits rest is a good practice. Unless there is a very good reason to call them, I will not bring her here for your entertainment."

Mrs. Mancos pressed her lips together looking displeased, but also contemplative. "I am not looking for some party trick, Mr. Abeyta," she said coldly. "My brother, Garrett, writes me emails or is calling me every day. He dreams of our cousin, Katrina. He's certain she is haunting him and believes her soul is not at rest. This year is the thirtieth anniversary of her disappearance. Garrett doesn't understand why she is coming to him now after all these years, but neither one of us question the ways of the Spirit World. He wants her found once and for all so he can sleep again. I think we would all rest easier if we could find out what happened to her."

"We?" Chris asked, hearing the implication that more than the two of them were involved.

Mrs. Mancos fiddled with her fingers, her iced tea forgotten and sweating on the table. After a pause, she looked up to meet Chris's gaze straight on.

"My husband, Billy, was with my brother and I the day Katrina disappeared in the mountains on a camping trip. The three of us were the last people to see her alive. Well, as far as we know."

"And what happened to your cousin, Mrs. Mancos?"

She drummed the fingers of one hand on the table. "Will you please call me Patricia?"

He could feel her hesitating to answer and could see the somber cloud building around her and altering her aura. "I can call you Patricia if you like." He cleared his throat. "If you want my help you must tell me what you know. I cannot be expected to help Katrina if I do not know the circumstances regarding her disappearance. Are you certain she is deceased?"

A flat expression replaced Patricia's previous look of distress. "Her body was never found, Mr. Abeyta. That's all I can tell you. We were young and misguided and we—all four of us—made a mistake. I believe it cost my cousin her life."

"Tell me where she disappeared."

"It was near South Mineral Campground. Is it possible for her spirit to still reside on Earth, or in this plane of existence, even after all these years?"

"It is possible," Chris said as he watched Patricia's aura closely. Her guard was up and Chris could see it like an iron gate around her. The woman was letting Chris in just enough for him to see the entrance of her wall of protection and peek inside, but he sensed there was much more to this situation. "Ghosts have no real sense of time. There are circumstances where a spirit in a state of unease will never depart the premises of an unfortunate event."

Patricia sat still as stone for a heavy moment. Chris decided to fill the empty space with a few of his own questions.

"Why did your brother not call me if he is the one having problems?"

His voice seemed to shake Patricia out of her silence.

"Garrett went to college out of state. Afterward, he was offered a job back east and he never came back. I don't blame him. There are virtually no jobs here. At least in his field. When the dreams started, he began telling me about them and asking me to drill Billy with all the same old questions from back then."

She shook her head as if to dispel the unpleasantness of the conversation.

"Why does he want *you* to question your husband? Why doesn't he ask him himself?"

She shrugged. It was two non-answers in a row. Chris didn't appreciate the deflection.

"Because he knows I have nothing new to tell him," a dark-haired, tall man said as he rounded the corner and entered the dining area of the kitchen.

Chris rose from his seat as the man stepped forward and held out his hand. Chris shook it. "Chris Abeyta," he said as way of an introduction.

"Billy Mancos," he said, and released Chris's hand. "Thanks for coming."

Billy moved behind Patricia and rested his hands on top of her shoulders.

"I'm Patricia's husband. I was the last person to see Katrina alive. Garrett is obsessed with her disappearance. He feels guilty about the whole mess and has for thirty years. I think the real reason he moved away is because if he lived here, he'd still be looking for her."

Patricia's mouth tightened with these words and she didn't disagree with him even though her explanation about Garrett's whereabouts had only to do with a job.

"Garrett's driving me crazy with all his emails and non-stop insistence that I find a private detective to re-open the case. I don't believe the cops and justice system will be able to help. The case is too old. Every resource available had already been exhausted with no success. You're our final attempt at finding out what really happened to my cousin."

"Tell me the whole story," Chris said to them both.

Billy took a seat next to his wife and they recounted their weekend excursion into the mountains three decades earlier.

"It happened at the end of a weekend camping trip with a bunch of friends. The four of us wanted to do some extra exploring before leaving the area. Katrina got all worked up about something. I can't even remember what it was now."

Patricia interrupted her husband. "My cousin became irrational over virtually nothing. She was acting like a spoiled child and went off to pout. Unfortunately she never came back."

Billy kept his eyes on his wife. He was tight-lipped, and Chris could feel the tension running through the man's bloodstream.

"We went after her, but she was gone. It's a horrible tragedy. We never meant to—"

Patricia cut off her husband again. "Katrina's parents were in the middle of a nasty divorce that summer. It's the reason they let her come stay with us for so long. I think her temper-tantrum the afternoon she disappeared had more to do with her unhappiness at home than whatever it is she was so upset about."

"What was she upset about?" Chris asked, looking for more clarification.

Maybe they expected each other to answer, but the resulting silence made Chris's suspicions deepen.

Patricia filled the gap. "Katrina wanted me to be a go-between for her and a boy she liked. I wouldn't do it. He was older and she was leaving to return home soon. I didn't see the point."

Chris studied her face and knew she held something back. He didn't like it, but he kept reminding himself he was here to find Katrina not badger the truth from these two.

Chris took a few notes, mostly about the location of the incident. Then he rose, shook their hands again, and held back his observations and comments about the undercurrent of deceit and guilt in the room. Accusations wouldn't help him find Katrina and if he made any incorrect assumptions, he could severely jeopardize the case. "I will do everything I can to bring harmony to your cousin's spirit," he told them, and left to find the ghost of a sixteen-year-old girl.

Chapter Three

THE NEXT MORNING, Chris woke at dawn and packed up his truck with the gear he needed to find Katrina Caldwell. He drove a couple of hours from his cabin before turning off the pavement and onto the road that led to South Mineral Campground. His directions were to pass the campground and follow South Mineral Creek until the road ended at a trailhead. From there he had directions that were supposed to take him somewhere below the north face of Rolling Mountain and due east. It was a regular occurrence for him to not take directions at one-hundred percent accuracy from nearly everyone. The way people explained how to get somewhere usually frustrated him, especially when it came to following forest service roads through the mountains. He figured Spirit would guide him when the time came if he were meant to assist on the case.

The truck rumbled over another washed out section of road and he clung to the steering wheel as he maneuvered and bounced over what appeared to be a dry stream bed. When he arrived, there were already a few vehicles at the parking area. He had never been to this particular spot before, but he knew this trailhead led to a few Colorado mountain summits that ranked as a 14er or 13er and it was a popular hiking destination.

His directions from Patricia were to stay on the east trail for half of a mile or until he reached the south branch of Mineral Creek. She believed that was the closest spot where officials had lost Katrina's trail thirty years earlier. He double-checked his hiking pack, slipped the straps over his shoulders and set out.

As the sun reached its peak in the sky, Chris felt the nagging sensation of being inside a hollow chasm. He continued hiking deeper into a narrow forested valley and couldn't shake the feeling. His heightened extrasensory perception picked up on absolutely nothing. Clark's nutcrackers followed him, chatting and begging for something to eat. The nuthatches and squirrels scurried about in the trees, their tiny feet scratching and crackling against the brittle bark of the pines. He stopped next to a runoff stream and knew he'd been duped by the Mancoses.

If the information he'd been given held even a crumb of truth, a niggling of his sixth sense should have been triggered by now. He took a drink from his water bottle and tucked it back into the side pocket of his pack. There were two scenarios he had to consider at this point. One, Katrina did not travel in this direction. If she had, nothing of consequence related to her disappearance happened along this route. Or two, Patricia gave him bogus directions on where to find the missing girl. If number two was correct, then number one was as well.

Chris turned around and headed back to his truck. He didn't like being lied to and couldn't understand why someone would pay him to hike around in the woods for no reason. He set his mind to determination level ten—the highest level. He would find out the facts behind this case. A raven cawed from far off to the west. It was a good sign that this new direction would lead him to what he wanted.

Back inside his truck, Chris dug out his cell phone and switched it on. No otherworldly messages waited for him this time. He wasn't surprised, but thought it would be convenient if the stupid phone could send him text messages from Great Spirit and save him a lot of time and hassle.

As suspected, the phone had no service in such a remote location. He needed to make a call before exploring any more of the surrounding area. He could easily spend the next year of his life climbing the peaks and looking in every valley and crevice for a hint of a sign from a lost spirit. There had to be a better way to narrow down which direction to look for Katrina.

He retraced his path as he drove over the rough, washed-out forest road and returned to the pavement. From there, he turned north, knowing there was a small town not too far away and hopefully had an ever-present cell tower.

When he knew he was a couple of miles from the old mining town—now rehabilitated into a tourist destination—he checked his phone for reception. Two bars meant he could make a call. He found a spot to pull over and called Patricia Mancos. Taking the bull by the horns and being direct was the only way he operated, at least at first.

It was no shock when she or Billy didn't answer. Chris pulled out his notebook and proceeded with plan B.

It took him three calls to find Garrett Sanchez in Lexington, Kentucky.

The man answered and Chris could immediately tell that Patricia's brother spoke on a cell phone. The sound quality was akin to speaking to someone through a screen of angry bees while driving a dump truck.

"Hello? This is Chris Abeyta from Colorado," he said again for the third time.

His blood pressure made the roof of his head feel like it was about to explode.

"What? Who?" Garrett asked again. "Give me a second. I can barely hear you."

Chris ground his molars and ruminated with disgust why he owned a cellular telephone. He wondered why anyone in their right mind owned one. He was sure the invention of the cell phone was the mark of the beginning of the end of human civility. Or maybe that had already happened long ago with the invention of the telegraph machine.

"I need to speak to you about Katrina Caldwell."

"Just a minute. I can't understand a thing you're saying," the man said in a chopped up and garbled voice.

Chris glared at his phone, pushed the speaker button, and waited impatiently.

The buzz and miscellaneous background noises lessened and Garrett finally spoke relatively clearly through the connection.

"Who'd you say this was?"

Chris cleared his throat. "My name is Chris Abeyta. I was hired by your sister, Patricia, to find your cousin, Katrina."

There was an empty pause and Chris immediately thought the call had been dropped. He lowered the window of his pickup truck and was about to hurl the phone out into the road to be run over by the next passing vehicle when he heard Garrett respond.

"Umm. Yeah. Right. How's everything going?"

"Not well. I need to ask you a few questions. Do you have a minute to talk?"

"Sure. I'm sorry about the bad connection. You caught me on the job. I work weird hours. I'm surprised you caught me."

"That's fine," Chris lied. He hated the spotty call, but he was grateful to have found the correct man with little trouble instead of having to wait a day or two to track him down. He was also glad he'd asked Patricia for her brother's full name and location. She had hesitated in giving him the information, but he'd told her that every detail mattered in cases like this. She'd given her brother's name and city and said her brother was unreachable by phone most days when he was on the job site. Garrett had just confirmed that so he knew Patricia hadn't lied about everything. Chris hadn't pushed for more information about Garrett during the interview thinking it was inconsequential or he could acquire it later if need be. Now was later and here he was seeking out the brother.

"Your sister and brother-in-law told me I needed to look for Katrina south and east of South Mineral Campground. I have looked in that area and found nothing of importance. Can you tell me anything more regarding the location of her disappearance?"

Chris waited through another lengthy pause.

"South and east? No. I don't think that's correct. Is that where Billy told you to start looking?"

"No. The information was given to me from your sister."

"Huh. Patricia must be confused. She never was good with directions. I'm sorry. I wish I was there with you, but I'm contracted out on this job and I can't leave until February. There will be too much snow up in the mountains by then and you'll never get in. Listen, Mr. Abeyta, these dreams I've been having about my cousin are keeping me from sleeping. They're dark and creepy. I'll be mostly asleep and then I'm frozen to the bone and surrounded with beating wings. Katrina's face will be in front of mine, or I'll hear her crying. This has to stop. If you can do anything to help, you'll be saving my sanity. I'm going totally crazy. It's going to cost me my job."

"I understand," Chris said. "But I can't do anything if I don't know where to begin looking."

"When you get to the parking area at the trailhead, head south for a quarter of a mile and then turn due west. Patricia must have said east, but she meant west."

Chris took more notes as he asked a few more questions. Garrett was a hundred percent more helpful than his sister, and he wondered again why Patricia had hired him instead of her brother.

"Why didn't you call me instead of having your sister do it?" he asked before ending the call.

"Oh, well," Garrett hesitated as if thinking about it. "Patricia offered to take care of it since she lives closer. She said she had heard of you and what you do as a ghost hunter. I thought she could handle it. I'm sure she just made a simple mistake with the directions. Call me anytime if you have any more questions. Actually, could you call me when and if you find my cousin?"

"Will do," Chris said and hung up.

* * *

Chris headed back to his starting point at the trailhead and climbed out of the truck once more. A few yards down the trail, he received a positive sign from Great Spirit as the normal easterly winds changed directions and blew southwest. The mountain grass swayed and rippled with the sudden strong breeze. The grasses, wildflowers and tree tops pointed directly at Rolling Mountain as if telling him he was now going the right way.

Twenty minutes later, Chris found a unique rock formation jutting out of the side of the mountain. Before venturing toward the rocks, he peered south and saw the collapsed and half rotted timbers of an old mining head frame about seventy-five yards away. He moved closer to the stone crags, crevices, and stacked boulders and believed he'd found the location of where Katrina resided. Nothing ghostly or undead spoke to him directly, but he could sense the presence of a spirit at unrest just as clearly as he could feel the light breeze brushing his skin. The gut feeling he was moving in the right direction was the usual sign he waited for when working a case. It never failed him. The area also matched Garrett's description—which was remarkably different than Patricia's version.

He searched and climbed over the rocks looking at them from different angles and perspectives. They loomed over him as if reaching out from the very core of the Earth seeking fresh air and blue skies. Jagged, crumbling stones with cliff faces and plunging crevices surrounded him. It took further investigating to find the exact location of where he could advance into the geological formation. After a few more minutes of searching, he found a place with decent footing and he began the descent. It was mildly daunting, but Chris was an experienced mountaineer and he wouldn't let a little rock-scrambling stop him. He wedged himself into a narrow crevice, using his arm strength and feet to keep him from falling straight down. He kept going until he reached the bottom and found a narrow passageway through the rocks. Ten yards further, he saw an opening in the rocks darker than a void.

Before entering, Chris squatted down and retrieved the implements of his trade from his backpack. The energy inside a cave could be either of light or darkness. He wouldn't know for sure until he was immersed in it. He had a feeling about this cave, but he wouldn't assume anything yet. The area was a historical mining district and that meant the possibility of many things regarding place energy. Lost souls and disgruntled deceased inhabitants could saturate the old mine and nearby forest with their discord. If a tragedy happened here, other than Katrina's disappearance, it would be difficult to discern her energy signature from someone else's. At least at first. He hoped the distant past with the mining didn't interfere with his search for the girl.

With so much to remain aware of, Chris smudged himself with sage, said his prayers of protection, and pulled out the small medicine bag he wore beneath his shirt so it was visible. He unpacked the raven feathers he'd collected the day before. They were now separated from the wing bones and nestled inside a leather bag along with one raven foot. He silently thanked the raven once more as he began the process of using the sacred objects for his own shamanic and spiritual purposes.

He unfolded the red cotton flannel and carefully removed the small bundle. The raven foot was wrapped with a string of multi-colored beads. He unwound the beads and the foot swung gently through the air. Chris rose to find a place in the rocks where he could hang it over the entrance. There was nothing to tie it to, so he found a loose stone and used the rock as a weight on the end of the string. The claws dangled in front of the cave entrance and Chris felt assured that the raven would protect him and guide him if the need arose.

He kept the bag of feathers close to hand as he slipped around the raven foot and entered the cave, his flashlight leading the way. Eight feet past the entrance the cave widened into an old mineshaft. It was pretty much what Garrett described to him, and after thirty years he guessed not much had changed other than the extra layers of dust. The timbers supporting the shaft looked undisturbed and as strong as the day they were installed. Chris removed a feather from the bag. He stuck the quill end of the feather into a crack on a support beam to his left so the feather stood straight out. Stopping every fifteen to thirty feet, he positioned another feather the same way, always sticking out so they were visible from one feather to the next by shining his flashlight.

After a few handfuls of feathers, he knew he had ventured far enough. The air inside the mineshaft altered and was somehow fresher, although it now carried a scent that reminded him of moss and lichens after a summer rain. Chris quit leaving a trail of raven feathers and hunkered down close to the floor. He waited and listened while keeping the flashlight pointing down so the ray of light was only a small pool around his boots.

Breathing in the cool air he knew water must be near even though he could not hear or see it.

"Katrina Caldwell, show yourself."

Silence answered, but the hair rising on his arms and the back of his neck spoke loudly enough.

"It is time to come forward and join your ancestors," he said, encouraging her but also commanding her.

Even being deep inside the mountain, an unnatural stillness settled around him. His breath stopped moving as he waited knowing this was the calm before the storm. A female energy came forward slowly, and then all at once. She darted by him and then disappeared again. The air moved like a soft whisper, touching his cheek and sending the scent of wet stone and damp ground. It lasted less than a second before a gust of wind picked up the century of dust inside the tunnel and blasted him in a whirlwind of violence.

She screamed and the sound echoed over the rocks and bounced back at him from all directions. Chris gripped the medicine bag that hung around his neck, closed his eyes, and held his breath. He distinctly felt her feminine energy and heard her voice shrieking.

"Noooo!" it rang through the tunnels. "I hate you! Go away!"

The disturbance upset the mountain. Sand, gravel, and small stones began to trickle down the walls and fall from the ceiling. Chris edged toward a support beam and huddled next to it until the screaming stopped and the wind settled. The last thing he wanted was to be buried in a cave-in. Chances were fairly good, if not a hundred percent, that if the mountain collapsed he would never be found. The idea didn't sit well on his shoulders. He regained his feet and stayed composed.

"Katrina, do not be frightened. Show yourself so I may help you."

"Not you!" she yelled back.

Chris set his jaw, determined to ferret her out of the mineshafts and settle this case. Great Spirit did not lead him here to fail. How he was going to succeed at this may be uncertain, but he wouldn't give up without trying his best.

"I call you forward. The ancestors implore you to join them. Great Spirit blesses this meeting."

"Not. You. Leave me alone!"

He got a glimpse of her and saw her blonde hair and long limbs. She wore jeans and a tank top, and he could even make out the tiny glint of her gold necklace in his flashlight beam. This time her words were followed by a loud crack and the earth shattering somewhere farther down the tunnel. Chris covered his face with his arm, breathing into his shirt sleeve as more dust rushed past him. A new sound added to the crumbling of rock and trickle of gravel. It started as a slight vibration but quickly turned into a rush that reminded him of water tumbling over loose stones at high speed. *Was he about to drown?* The idea was even worse than being crushed.

What followed next was almost pleasant compared to the idea of rising water. A colony of manic bats soared by him in a flurry of beating wings. They no doubt had been disturbed by the falling rock and shifting of the earth.

"You don't want me. You only want to trick me. Get out of here!" she screamed.

The bats disappeared down the tunnel and took with them his light. They didn't actually take it, the flashlight was still gripped in his palm, but with their passing the bulb went out. Chris thought he could actually feel the filament inside the tiny bulb burst with Katrina's anger.

He paused for the length of time it took to close his eyes and call silently to the spirit of the raven. With eyes open there was no difference in the absence of light within the mountain. Pure darkness was absolute in every direction. A poignant curse word teased the tip of his tongue, but he held it in with the knowledge that it would do no good. There was always a lesson to be learned in every situation and being confronted by a hostile spirit would surely teach him something new. He remained centered and focused, and peered in the direction from which he thought he had come.

Within a second he saw what he was looking for. The last raven feather he stuck into a support timber glowed a soft iridescent silver. Katrina was nowhere to be seen without his flashlight, but he thought he heard sobbing. Now that he had a better idea of what he was dealing with, he made the decision to return later and better prepared. Chris made his way slowly toward the feather and kept going from feather to feather until he reached the entrance once again. He retrieved his raven foot, wrapped the string of beads around it and packed it with the remaining feathers.

Before leaving, he acknowledged the raven magic he'd used with a reassuring pat of his hand on the bag. Then he glowered at the cave entrance with no little restiveness.

He climbed out of the crevice, over the rocks and hiked back to his truck formulating his next move.

Chapter Four

"COME WITH ME."

"Umm... How about a hello?"

Chris watched Juliana's brows stretch toward her hairline. She wanted him to play like a polite member of society, and make nice-nice with her, but she should know him better than that by now. He took her by the arm and pulled her onto the front porch. She stumbled out the door and out of his grip as he tried to escort her down the front steps.

"Hey, I know, how about not man-handling me and explaining what you're doing here."

"I need your help and you need to learn. It is a win-win for us both." He walked off the front porch expecting her to follow. When he didn't hear her steps echoing his, he sighed and turned back around. Juliana was not the type of person to follow someone blindly. She always had to have a hundred questions answered first.

Chris frowned and waited for the rapid fire interrogation to begin.

"So, you show up unannounced, grab me by the arm—without saying hello, might I add—and tell me it's time for a lesson on the Spirit World?"

Her eyebrow was cocked along with the corresponding side of her hip.

"Yes," he said, and steeled his resolve to wade through the morass of small talk. "This is not a problem, Juliana. You are my apprentice and it is time to go learn something of value." He looked her over. "You look good to go."

Incredulity and disbelief fluttered over her features. Chris understood she wanted more time to take in his request, but he believed she should get used to his way of working. There was no better way to adjust to a new situation than diving straight in.

He watched her swallow and lick her lips.

"Where are you taking me?"

"Ghost hunting. I have a case and I need a female."

"No, no, and no," she said stubbornly. "See this?" She pointed at all of herself.

He could tell she didn't expect him to answer.

"This is me departing on the nope train." She spun around and went directly for the front door. "It has a theme song too. It goes like this... Nope nope no. No way, no thank you, no how. Now go away and don't come back."

"Stop."

"I only hear you saying, *run away as fast as you can.*" She held one hand up as if to halt him, even though he hadn't moved from his spot in the driveway. Her other hand was pressed over her ear. She did stop retreating however.

He began to remind her of the many incidents that required his help without which she would have been in grave or mortal danger. "Juliana, I have saved you from spiritual possession, demons, spirits of an unfriendly nature, and death. I've protected your property which in turn kept you and your family from any number of devastating misadventures. Today, I am requesting your cooperation and the use of your climbing gear. If you choose not to—"

"Oh God," she said with a groan.

He watched her place her palm to her forehead and press.

"Fine. I'll come, but you should know I'm not the best translator for the dead," she said, trudging down the steps.

* * *

Juliana tied off and began her descent down the rock wall. The tension in the rope felt good. Secure but giving. He'd shown her where he'd descended the crevice with no gear and they'd promptly agreed to use her ropes. When her arm broke through the first sticky strings of spider web, she almost reversed direction and climbed back up. *Chris could manage this case without her!*

"Spiders are definitely not part of the deal," she said, and rethought his free climbing path to the bottom.

"They're harmless," he said down to her with his usual tone of impatience.

She clenched her teeth and took a shuddering breath through her nose. If Katrina's ghost was down here, didn't that mean her body was as well? A renewed sense of panic raced through her bloodstream, cold as ice, and chilled her to the bone. Chris thought he hadn't found the body when he was here the day before, but that didn't mean it wasn't there. In Juliana's opinion, it just meant he didn't see it.

What was she doing?! This is insane.

Even with the mental lecture haranguing her incessantly, she continued to walk herself into the deathtrap. It wasn't a deathtrap of course since she had the ropes and harnesses, but since her head was already playing games with her on this supernatural errand, she figured she may as well exaggerate it to the fullest.

Sunlight lit the crevice for a full twenty feet before the angle of the mid-day sun caught the edge of the rocks and cast a shadow against the stone wall. Chris swore the bottom was only about twenty-five to thirty feet down, so Juliana knew she was almost there as her head dipped below the line of light and fell into the shadows.

The repelling wasn't her biggest problem with this adventure. The crevice in the rock formation eventually came to an end, but that's where it met the old mineshaft. At some point in time the ground must have caved in and exposed the tunnels adjacent to and below the rocks. Cave-ins and shifting earth were a somewhat common problem in the area and warning signs about opens shafts were posted along roadways and all over in these mountains. Juliana knew that even after a century or longer, sinkholes and old mines could appear in the forest at any time and to anyone's demise.

Chris gave her his word that he'd already scouted the path and it was safe.

She reached the bottom, unclipped and tugged the rope twice. "Your turn, Chief."

Chris joined her a few minutes later. "Have we ever discussed your nickname for me?"

"Hmm," Juliana tapped her chin with a long delicate finger and looked up at her hairline while trying not to smirk. "No. I don't believe we have, Chief."

He rolled his eyes, or at least Juliana considered it an eye roll even if Chris's expression barely changed.

"It's Chris. Chief is inappropriate on many levels. Number one being I hold no position in the tribal council."

"Alrighty then. If you insist on Chief Chris, I suppose I can start using that instead. Hey, how about Chief Christopher or Chief Abeyta?"

She thought she may have heard a growl rumble out of him as he passed by her, but he otherwise didn't reply to her teasing. She wriggled her shoulders to help settle her backpack and followed after him continuing to amuse herself with more name play.

"Is your name Christopher? How about Christian? Now that would be ironic. What's your middle name anyway? I bet you have a really cool secret Native name. I mean the name Chris is so common. What were your parents thinking when they gave you an Anglo name? Not that I should talk. I'm Juliana Katherine, but then again, I'm half Irish so it's not a huge surprise that I don't have a Native name." She paused to catch her breath.

This time she definitely heard a growl coming from Chris. "Listen, Ant, if you could stop babbling for one minute, I might be able to answer one of your questions."

"See right there. You called me Ant again. That is the reason I call you Chief. Seriously, Chief. If I have to have a ridiculous nickname, then so do you."

Chris's mouth turned down farther than she thought was humanly possible. She enjoyed tormenting him in these simple ways. It was just too easy. Running her mouth would guarantee Chris's disapproval, but hey, he was the one who dragged her out here to go ghost hunting and do other things that were probably going to be even worse. She wasn't a fan of her current situation and talking helped keep her mind off of what they were doing.

Juliana lifted her brows and waited. Chris remained silent. She couldn't take it. "So, what is it? Which of my questions are you going to answer?"

"It's just Chris. My middle name is of no importance right now and that's all you get until you do what you came here to do."

"Then after I talk to your timid ghost girl you'll tell me the rest?"

"We'll see," he said.

She narrowed a green eye at him and stopped traversing over the uneven rocks. The opening to the abandoned mine lay directly in front of Chris. He switched on his headlamp and handed her a second one.

"She will speak with you," he said sounding altogether more confident than Jules felt. "Once I know we're near her, I'll hang back. You can stop any time you want, but if you can find out what happened thirty years ago, it will be good for everyone involved."

"Let me paraphrase one last time before I go in, just to make sure I'm not missing anything. You say she's hiding inside and is violent toward you, but you think she'll be fine with me because I pose no threat?"

He nodded soberly.

"And I need to find out how she died because she's haunting some dude's dreams in Kentucky?"

"Yes."

"And I'm doing this because I have nothing better to do on a Thursday afternoon and I totally love talking to dead people."

"Your sarcasm is not lost on me but we are running out of time. I don't know how you feel about climbing and hiking in the dark."

"I don't know how I feel about it either because I've never done it before."

"Then let's go in so we don't also have that experience today."

She let out a little huff. "You know, I already consider you using guilt to make me come up here with you objectionable."

"There is no guilt. You are doing what you need to do, as am I."

"Whatever," she said with defiant indifference. "If this girl freaks me out, I'm high-tailing it back to the truck."

Chris smudged them both with sage and sweetgrass, sprinkled his sacred corn pollen on her head and on his tongue and prayed for them. He hung what looked like a bird foot over the entrance to the mine and went inside. Juliana scooted around the dead animal part and tried to ignore it, and her distaste for such things. Chris's tools of his profession were not to be questioned or judged. He'd helped her in more ways than she could list with all kinds of problems involving spirits and supernatural entities. Just because she thought animal parts were gross, didn't mean they weren't beneficial for his shamanism. She prayed her lessons with Chris wouldn't involve dismembering anything that had a heartbeat and so far she hadn't experienced anything of the sort.

Broken stones littered the floor and she stepped carefully over and around them until she was past the entrance and swallowed by the dark. She swept the beam of her headlight left and right and up and down taking in the old timbers and hoped today wouldn't be the day they collapsed. "Do you have life insurance?" she asked.

"No."

"Neither do I," she said, not withholding her irritation and uncertainty.

"You are in my circle of protection. Now be quiet and focus."

She sucked in a long breath and realized the dusty air tasted weird, bitter, and not good. The smell vaguely reminded her of the bottom of her brother, Jared's, clothes hamper. She shut her mouth and continued forward taking shallow breaths through her nose.

"I'll tell you when to call her if you do not feel her presence. You will not be able to see me until I am ready for her."

"What are you talking about, Chief?"

"Go slowly. When it's time, say her name. She will come."

Juliana's pace slowed to nearly a stop. *How was she going to be able to do this?* She decided she needed a theme song. Something that would give her the courage she was severely lacking. Something that lightened her mood by a thousand percent. She scrunched up her face and squeezed her brains. *Geez!* For the life of her she couldn't remember how the Ghostbusters song went. She pinched her arm thinking it would distract her mind enough to remember it. *Urghh.* The only thing that came to mind under the pressure of wanting to actually use her mind's catalog of music, lyrics, and other assorted theme songs was Scooby Doo. It was ridiculous but also helping. She hummed under her breath and said the lyrics in her head…*Scooby Doobie Doo, where are you…* It went on and her feet carried her forward. Chris didn't remark at the humming, but he did grace her with another irritable "Chief Chris" look.

The feeling came over her with a solid whump. There was no ignoring it. Juliana knew she'd entered Katrina's territory by the heavy coldness to the air and the unusual scent. If anything reached out of the darkness and touched her she would keel over and die. She just knew it. It'd be a simple death. Heart attack. *No biggie.* But, she vowed she'd haunt Chris for the rest of eternity. She'd ask him ridiculous and pointless questions until he brought her back from the dead. *Could he do that?*

She mustered up her courage, took a drink of water from her bottle and then called for the girl. "Katrina, are you in here?"

Chris had warned her he would be unseen once they neared Katrina. Juliana didn't believe he had actually disappeared, but then again…he was Chris Abeyta and his shamanism was pretty much a complete mystery to her.

Katrina came forward only slightly less timid than a mouse. The hairs on Jules's body rose like miniature supernatural sensors. Katrina Caldwell appeared to be a typical teen-aged girl. She was thin, small-chested, and tallish. Her dark blonde hair hung just below her shoulders and she looked like she'd been crying.

Juliana worked her lips back and forth before finding her voice again. Did she really owe Chris a favor? She wasn't totally convinced this was worth a trade for all Chris had done for her. Okay, so that was a lie. Chris had saved her life and her soul. Yes, she owed Chris, which is the only reason she stood in this dark, dank, musty, and dusty mineshaft.

"Why are you in here?"

Katrina retreated a few steps.

"Sorry," she said hurriedly, afraid the girl would leave. "I meant...Hi, I'm Jules. You doing okay? You look a little upset."

"I'm not so great. How did you get in here?" she asked, and came fully into the circle of light.

"I'm here exploring the old mine. What about you?"

She shrugged and peered down the mineshaft back the way she'd come.

"Do you know how I can get out of here?" Juliana asked, in an attempt to keep the girl talking.

Chris suggested if she could get Katrina's story, it could really help the case. Ghosts often hold onto their trauma. Getting it out of them can make a huge difference in helping them cross over. Juliana wasn't sure if she wanted to know the sordid details, but she was here to help Chris. And now that Katrina was right in front of her, she began to feel sympathy for the girl instead of scared out of her wit's end.

"It's that way," Katrina said, pointing her finger. "I got turned around in here once, but my friends knew how to find the exit."

"Yeah? What were you and your friends doing? Were you out having fun or something?"

Katrina glanced around again and a slightly thoughtful look crossed her face. "We've been camping. It was a normal weekend for my cousins and their friends, but since I'm here visiting from the city, it's all new and thrilling for me."

"Did you camp at the campground down the mountain from here? It's a nice place. I like the stream."

"Yeah, I like it too. It's been a great weekend. Well, until the end."

Juliana tried to smile, but it felt forced and awkward. She noticed the dark line on Katrina's arm and thought it looked like a cut. She didn't mention it yet.

"What happened to make you say it like that? I mean, the 'until the end' part?" Juliana was fairly certain Katrina didn't know she was dead. It was awful to think, but she had a strong feeling it was true.

"There was like ten of us camping this weekend. All teenagers and no parents. It was pretty great." She settled down next to the wall opposite Jules and crossed her legs. As she began to tell her story, she traced her finger around in the dusty floor of the tunnel. "My cousin Garrett and his best friend, Billy, managed to get a couple cases of beer for the weekend. They thought it was the greatest thing since the invention of the wheel. I thought it tasted like warm piss, but I drank it anyway. I didn't want them to think I was lame. It was totally wasted on me because I didn't even catch a buzz."

"So you went camping, but how did you end up inside an old mine?"

"Billy knew a place where you could get into the tunnels. He said he found it on a camping trip with his parents. He never told anyone about it because he knew his parents would freak out and forbid him to go inside. On the second day of the camping trip, he showed Garrett, Patricia and I the spot. He didn't want the other kids knowing about it. I don't remember the reason why, but I remember feeling really special that he let me in on the secret."

Jules's mind immediately jumped to how suspicious that sounded, but she kept quiet and let Katrina continue.

"We didn't go through the entrance the first time. No one had a flashlight or anything, but the four of us made plans to come back the next day after the rest of the group left. We hiked back to our campsite and spent the rest of the day messing around. The guys fished or threw the football around and Patricia and I hung out and talked. I think we waded in the stream in our bikini tops and shorts and hoped the guys were checking us out. Later, we just chilled out by the fire and ate s'mores and marshmallows. I told her how much I liked Billy and I tried to convince her to drop a hint to him and see if he had any interest in me. She wouldn't do it no matter how much I begged. I got really frustrated and told her she was being a crappy cousin."

"Why wouldn't she help you?"

Katrina shrugged and looked down at her shoes. "She was pretty vague at first, but then she said she didn't want to get in the middle of it."

"What did you do after that?"

"I don't know. Not much. I pretended like I wasn't watching him every second. Then after dinner I tried to joke around and flirt with him. He was nice to me, but mostly he was into drinking the horrible beer and burping the alphabet with the guys."

Jules managed to keep her eyes from rolling—barely—and didn't remark on how unattractive Billy sounded.

"We went to sleep late that night and all I did was lay awake and wish he would sneak into my tent. I even wondered if I should try to sneak into his, but I knew my cousin, Garrett, would be pissed off and probably tell my mom. He always acts like my older brother when I come to visit. I eventually fell asleep with the knowledge that the next day would just be the four of us and then maybe I could tell Billy in private how much I loved him."

"Are you in love with him?" Jules asked. She couldn't help but notice how Katrina went from using the word like to the word love.

Katrina smiled as if she couldn't contain her happiness. It weirded Jules out. She couldn't understand how a sixteen-year-old girl could fall in love with a guy who showed little to no interest in return. She highly suspected Katrina's true feelings toward Billy were more in the range of intense infatuation and not really love, but Katrina was probably too young to understand the difference. How Jules understood this when she was only a few years older didn't exactly make sense even in her own mind. Many things regarding age and the wisdom that supposedly came with it didn't apply to her. Chris was the same way. It was likely one of the reasons they were friends. *Birds of a feather....* When it came to her and Chris, it was more like *weirdos* of a feather flock together. In the long and the short of it, she was all right with her strangeness. *Who wanted to be normal anyway?*

"We went back to the mine entrance after the rest of our group packed up and headed back to town. We told everyone we wanted to go for a hike before leaving. The four of us were riding in one vehicle anyway. Three of us were cousins and Billy was Garrett's best friend. No one questioned us.

"We only had two flashlights so the girls carried one and the guys carried the other one. We started down the first tunnel and I was pretty excited. I'd never been deep inside the ground before. I was a little nervous, but I didn't admit it. We found one collapsed passageway and had to turn around. Then we found a shaft that dropped straight down and that scared me a little. Billy and Garrett were walking in front of us and I thought about how easy they could have walked straight over the edge and been gone. That's about the time I decided I'd had enough exploring and I asked if we could go back out."

She rubbed at her temples and I watched a range of emotions play across her face. Katrina glanced around the tunnel and then continued after she seemed more in control of herself.

"Garrett started making fun of me. He teased me for being scared and said I was too young and should have waited in the Jeep Wagoneer. He compared me to his sister and said Patty wasn't acting like a baby. It infuriated me. Patricia—I always call her Patty—laughed at his jokes and added a couple of her own. Then he switched off his flashlight and Patty did too. I took a step back and stumbled. I thought I was going to fall down the shaft and die. Instead I fell into the wall and scraped my arm. It hurt bad and I could feel the cuts and the blood. I couldn't stop the tears from starting.

"Billy spoke up then and told Garrett he should quit acting like an asshole and to switch the light back on.

When they saw the cut on my arm, he looked like he felt bad about his teasing. He even apologized and said we should head out of the mine.

"It didn't turn out as great as I thought it should have. My arm stung and I was worried we wouldn't be able to find our way out. I mean, we didn't exactly leave a trail of bread crumbs or anything. In the end we really only made a few turns and we were back at the entrance in what seemed like no time."

"So you guys went in, fooled around, and then left. All that happened to you is a scrape on your arm?" Juliana asked, feeling like Katrina wasn't telling everything.

"Yeah. I wanted to pull Billy aside the entire time and tell him how much he meant to me and then hopefully kiss him in the dark but I never got the chance. That part really sucked."

"If you left with your cousins and Billy, how did you end up back here?"

"We made it to the entrance without any problem. I was really surprised to see how late in the day it was. We must have been wandering around inside for a couple of hours which would explain why I was feeling tired and my feet were sore. As we started back to Garrett's Wagoneer I realized my necklace was missing. I pretty much freaked out. It was a fourteen carat gold locket on a chain that my parents gave me. It meant everything to me. As soon as I noticed it was gone, I knew it came off when I tripped and fell. I must have felt it come off, but I was too panicked to pay attention at the time.

"Anyway, I told them to stop and I had to go back inside for my locket.

"Garrett said he wasn't going back in. He was hungry and tired of dragging two whiny girls around with him all day. Patty punched him on the arm and said something about not calling her whiny. She didn't want to go back inside the mine either.

"I started crying again. I couldn't leave it behind. It was the most valuable thing I owned and my parents were having a rough time. I couldn't leave Colorado without it. I asked for the flashlight and Garrett handed one over. He said he'd wait for me but he wasn't going with me.

"I really didn't want to make the trek back inside by myself, but I was determined and I would if I had to. Thankfully, Billy stepped up and said he would go with me.

"I was thrilled. I was also tired but it meant everything to me that Billy would come with me. Then Patty said she was going inside too. I was surprised how she suddenly changed her mind, but by that point, I just wanted to find my necklace. I was still a little disappointed I wouldn't be alone with Billy."

"Okay, so you retraced your steps and then what?" Juliana asked.

"We started backtracking. Garrett said he'd wait for us. I apologized because he was so grumpy and I knew by the time we went back in and came out again it was going to be dark out. The hike to the Wagoneer was close to an hour long walk. I said we'd return as quickly as possible and the three of us went after my locket. Right before we turned into the next tunnel we heard a noise. I had no idea what it could be. None of us knew. It was like wind blowing dry leaves or water rushing over gravel. It didn't make sense, but all of a sudden we found out what it was. Bats started leaving the mine. Patty flipped out. She waved her arms around, swatting at them like she was fighting them off. She was shrieking and out of control. I tried to get her to crouch down and wait for them to pass, but she wouldn't calm down. The bat colony was unsettling, with their flapping wings in the dark, but her reaction was way worse. When they petered out, Billy walked Patricia back to the entrance and then we went in for my necklace.

"I was finally alone with him."

She looked Juliana in the eyes and she didn't want to see the look on Katrina's face. It was happy and sad, but mostly heartbreaking. Somewhere in this story, her end was coming. Juliana felt it like a weight on her chest.

"At first we just walked, shining the light on the ground so we didn't trip over rocks or step in the guano. We were both listening for more bats, but there was only the occasional stray after the colony had left.

"I silently took his hand in mine and I about died of happiness when he let me hold it and didn't pull away. After a few minutes I said, 'This is nice.' and lifted our hands up a few inches. That's when he took his hand back.

"'I'm sorry Katrina, you're too young for me. You're still in high school and I don't date high school girls anymore.'"

"I got angry and said, 'Billy, you're only a few years older than me. When you're twenty-three and I'm twenty it won't make any difference at all.'"

"He said, 'But right now you're sixteen and I'm nineteen and it does matter.'"

"'Hardly,' I fumed back at him."

"'Don't Katrina. You're my best friend's cousin and it makes everything awkward. Just stop it.'"

"'I can't stop. I've never felt like this before about anyone. I think you like me too and you won't admit it. I've seen you watching me this weekend.'

"We kept walking as we talked. I was upset but trying to sound calm. I heard him sort of sniff at my declaration and I peered up at him in the semi-dark. He wouldn't look at me.

"He said, 'You're wrong, Katrina. I haven't been looking at you. Not like that.'

"'What's that supposed to mean?'"

"'It means I like someone else.' He paused and then added, 'Let's find your locket and get out of here, okay?'"

"'Who?' I demanded and stopped walking. I wanted to know what girl had stolen Billy's attention away from me. I wanted to know if I knew her, or if Patty did, so I could see her for myself."

"'It's no one you have to be concerned about. Drop it, Katrina. Don't make me regret coming all the way in here with you.'"

"I pouted and stayed silent as we turned the last corner and walked toward where I was sure my locket would be on the ground. I asked him for the flashlight. At first he didn't want to hand it over, but I kept holding my hand out until he passed it to me. It was kind of stupid for us to let Patty take one of the flashlights outside with her, but we were all a little shaken up by the bats and we were in a hurry.

"I guess I shouldn't have done what I did next, but I wanted him to know how I really felt. I kept thinking if I could just kiss him then he would kiss me back and it would be perfect and he would forget about the other girl and go out with me.

"I clicked the flashlight off. I heard him stop walking. You wouldn't believe how dark it is in here without any light. It's darker than anything you can imagine. A total void. You can't even see your hand in front of your face."

With that, Juliana's head lamp went out. She froze and forced herself not to panic. Katrina was only playing some twisted game and she knew if she overreacted she could hurt herself. Juliana reached for her pack and began to slide it off her back so she could find the backup flashlight inside.

"Katrina, I don't need to see the darkness to know how inky black it is. Can you bring the lights back up now?"

Katrina faded into view as if she glowed from within. She was a pale grayish-blue and the only thing Juliana could see inside the mineshaft.

"I reached for Billy in the dark and asked him to kiss me," she said solemnly. "I told him it would be only the one time and I would never bring it up again. He didn't tear my hand away from his shirt like I thought he might. I flipped the flashlight on so I could see his face. He looked kind of indifferent, but I thought that was better than being mad at me.

"'Once, and then you drop it. Forever. I don't want to date you, Katrina.'"

"I didn't answer. I leaned up and pressed my lips to his. I'm pretty sure he liked it, but then I took it farther and cupped him between the legs. He backed away, but I pursued him and held onto his belt. He forced me to let go.

"'No! You're crazy. Stay away from me, Katrina Caldwell.'

"I threw the flashlight at him and yelled, 'You liked it and you know it!'

"The flashlight hit his stomach and then fell to the ground. My breath caught in my throat as I realized that I probably just broke it, but I didn't, and my shoulders sank with relief when the light stayed on.

"Billy was so angry. He starting telling me I was a crazy bitch and was backing away. I knew he liked me and I couldn't understand why he wouldn't admit it. I snatched the flashlight from the floor and turned to search the last section of the shaft to find my locket. I thought I saw it in the beam of light and started for it.

"I walked away from him and said something like I was going to tell Garrett and Patricia he kissed me and felt me up as soon as we were alone together. I'm not sure why I threatened him but he took it seriously and said, 'Screw you. You will not, because I'll tell them what you did and they'll believe me because I'm not a bat-shit crazy girl.'

"Then he was gone. I saw him walking away holding up a lighter he must have had in his pocket. I picked up my locket, saw the broken clasp, and put it in my pocket. I sat down and started to cry. Billy broke my heart and I needed a minute to calm down. I was sure he would come back for me when his finger started to burn from holding the lighter, or he would at least call back to me so I knew he was at the other end of the tunnel. I'm still waiting for him to come back."

Juliana blinked and felt mildly stunned. She had stopped searching for her backup light and watched Katrina's unearthly blue glow instead. She really didn't understand she was dead? How had she gone from crying in the dark cold tunnel to being a deceased teenager? Jules reached up tentatively and flipped the switch on her headlamp. Nothing happened. She hit it again and the light came back on.

"How long have you been in here?" she asked.

"I don't know. Maybe an hour or two."

"And you never thought to go after him?"

"I think I tried, but I got confused. The bats returned and I fell down when one flew in my face. I don't know. It kind of hurt."

"What hurt?" Juliana asked with caution.

"When I fell."

"Where's your flashlight?"

Katrina glanced around, looking baffled.

"Would you like to go outside with me now?"

"Billy is coming back. Even if he doesn't want to date me, I know he's a decent guy. He wouldn't leave me in here to die!"

She sounded defensive and her anger was rising. Juliana leaned back to put more space between her and the ghost. Her hand slid a few inches across the gravel and dirt floor of the rocky passageway and then went right over a ledge.

"Whoa!" she screamed and flung herself forward away from the chasm.

Katrina jumped up from her spot on the ground and eyed Juliana like she was a leper.

"There's a drop off right there," she said, shining the beam of her light on the spot.

It wasn't visible at first because of the way the timbers and the rock walls cast their shadows on that part of the tunnel. It was also partly hidden by an overhang of rock. She looked closer and could see the opening wasn't another tunnel. It was large enough to crawl into, or maybe squat down and peer inside, or maybe accidentally fall into. An icy shiver raced over her skin as she thought about Katrina sitting down to have a good cry over a boy who refused to return her affections, had a bat fly into her face...and accidentally slipped into the small tunnel.

"There are shafts like that all over this part of the mine. They're drains or air vents or something. You have to be really careful. Some are covered with metal grates but others are open traps. Like that one," Katrina said thoughtfully.

Juliana swallowed hard and could feel the knot of anxiety in the pit of her stomach churning. She wanted Chris to intervene like right now. She didn't know if she could convince Katrina thirty years had passed and it was time to leave the mine once and for all.

"So how about I lead you out and we can talk about something other than Billy. It may help to get your mind off of him."

Katrina frowned and rubbed at her forehead. "Did you see him when you came in?"

"Err...no. My friend and I didn't see anyone."

"What friend?" she asked sounding suspicious.

"His name is Chris. Can I ask him to join us?"

"I don't think that's such a great idea."

"I don't understand you right now. Chris is my friend and he may be able to help you."

"I don't need help. I'm waiting for Billy to see what a huge mistake he made and come back for me."

"Okay, well..." Juliana bit her lip and tried to think of how she could get through to this obsessive love-struck teen. She went back a few steps. "You said you were hurt. Chris is a doctor of sorts. You should let him look you over. Billy wouldn't want you to be injured and suffering."

Juliana could hardly believe how much she was playing along with this lunacy. *What the heck was she supposed to be learning anyway?* Chris had some serious explaining to do about her "lesson" on the paranormal—whether he wanted to talk about it or not.

"Billy sent me in here to help you." Chris spoke from the shadows and Juliana jumped out of her skin. She gripped the wall, well away from the air vent, and held in the shriek of surprise.

Katrina rushed forward toward the sound of Chris's voice. The blurred shape of her stretched ghostly body buzzed by Jules.

"Liar," she hissed into the dark.

Juliana heard the rattle and felt a vibration begin to thrum in the air. Chris forewarned her of the bats that lived here and she suspected they would be making an appearance any second now.

"He's not lying, Katrina," she said as she started edging toward the exit. "I swear to you. Billy and your cousins are desperate to find you."

"Billy?" Katrina said with hope tingeing her voice.

"That's right," she said. "They want you to come out of the mine now."

Juliana watched the pale shadow of Katrina's spirit stop advancing down the tunnel. Her eyes were trained on Jules's face and she tried her best to calm her features. Lying wasn't Juliana's strong point. She knew her face gave her away every time. She hadn't actually told a lie and this helped tremendously. In all honesty, she really didn't know if it would make any difference in this situation or not. Katrina was obviously confused by her current circumstances and if she assumed Patricia and Billy were waiting for her outside, that was all the better.

"They're outside?"

"It is time to come with us, Katrina Caldwell. Your friends are waiting for you," Chris said, and slid out of the dark and stood at the edge of the circle of light.

He was little more than an outline with the edges of his white T-shirt glowing in the dark. She swallowed and sweat began to dampen her body. The rattling flutter had settled from the deeper end of the mineshaft, but she knew the bats could erupt in a shower of frenzied wings at any minute.

She watched Katrina take a few steps toward Chris and then stop again.

"Why doesn't Billy come inside himself? Why did you bring this girl here?"

She looked back and forth between us, confusion and uncertainty morphing her expression. A sneer curled the side of her lip. "You're lying to me. Both of you are fat stinking liars!"

Chris jumped into the pool of light and threw something powdery at Katrina. The ghost screamed as she flew to the back of the tunnel.

Juliana heard Chris grunt with frustration. She suspected his trap had failed. Then Chris's boots pounded past her as he went after Katrina. She swung around and shined the light at him as he pursued the retreating ghost.

"Cowardice will get you nowhere fast, Katrina. Now is the time to face your fears. I call now for the help of the magpies! He tossed another handful of what looked like sticks and dirt mixed with black and white feathers into the dark ahead of him.

Juliana watched with equal horror and awe. The roar that followed Chris's actions was a mix of unearthly feminine screaming and of the stone and earth rumbling in protest to being disturbed.

"Get down!" Chris yelled.

Juliana hit the ground, flat on her stomach. She shielded her head and face by wrapping her arms tightly around her head. A squeak of fright escaped from her lips as she hugged the ground. The bats descended the tunnel. Chris told her the colony which lived here wasn't large and she had been stupid enough to believe him. It sounded and felt like a million bats the size of bullfrogs were swarming over and around her body.

Juliana had no idea how she survived through the horror of those passing minutes, but she somehow managed. When she heard or sensed Chris run past her, a part of her instantly realized she was being left behind.

When the flapping of wings and scraping of miscellaneous bat parts ceased, she rose from the floor and found her light still on. This helped marginally to stabilize her frantic heartbeat. There was no way in Hades she would stay behind in this haunted place alone. In one second flat, she gathered her wits, which were scattered from the mineshaft to Neptune, and ran after Chris.

Chapter Five

"STAND HERE AND don't move," Chris ordered as he shoved a talisman in Juliana's hands. "Hold this. If she tries to pass by you for the mine opening, raise it into her face."

He barked the directions at her and prayed she wasn't so terror-stricken she couldn't follow them. Juliana had made it safely out of the crevice without his help, but by the color of her complexion, a shade worse than puke-white, he didn't hold much hope for her assistance. In truth, he no longer really needed it. She'd done what he needed her to do. But he didn't want her presence to hinder his work and she was still somewhat better than having no assistant at all if she could hold it together.

Chris turned his back to Juliana and continued the process of moving Katrina's spirit from this plane of existence to the next one. The resistance of this teen-aged girl's will to remain planted inside the mine was pushing Chris's limits of patience. His determination not to fail surpassed his urge to throw his hands in the air and walk away from the case.

The cuts and scrapes over his face and arms stung and itched. Katrina's bats had done a number on his exposed skin. He was sure he appeared ghastly, which might help explain the grimace glued to Juliana's face. The blood trickling down his cheek would have to wait. The time to aid Katrina was right now, not after he took a five minute time out to nurse his wounds.

He centered his attention on the swirling mass of willow and aspen twigs, red clay powder, and magpie feathers. In the center of the commotion, Katrina rotated as if on a vertical spit. He'd trapped her and let the bats carry her out of the abandoned mine, away from the rocks and into the forest.

Synchronicity and signs had led him to this case and he felt it appropriate and ironic that Katrina had bonded so well with her bat companions. For Chris, the symbolization of bats was a constant reminder to Katrina to face her fears. She needed to discriminate what others told her and look for the truth behind the lies and stories her cousins and Billy had told her. Chris understood that even when Great Spirit sends a message, one must be able to recognize it. Katrina's mental instability made it difficult, or impossible, for the girl to understand the bats were there to help with transition and letting go. He wanted to help her navigate away from the dark and into a better place, but he had to act fast.

Katrina struggled against her restraints. Her spirit flailed and thrashed. Luckily the red clay dirt within the spiritual bonds had formed a nice paste over the girl's mouth. It resulted in a lot less screaming and cursing. The twigs and feathers whipped through the air like a cyclone and Chris kept back so as to not disturb the vortex.

"Ravens of the forest, I ask for your assistance now!" He let out a couple loud quarks followed by few long guttural croaks.

A raven answered his call and satisfaction trickled down his vertebrae when he saw the black bird circle over the treetops. If one raven came to him, he felt confident others would follow.

He bent down to his pack, stashed at the base of a pine tree and retrieved his hand drum. When he stood back up, he heard Katrina grunting and working her jaw against the clay within the confines of her rotating prison.

Ravens swooped overhead and coasted from tree to tree. Chris began to beat the drum in preparation for the ceremonial song which would help lift Katrina out of the heaviness of this dimension. It was the beginning of the process of opening a path for her soul to take. The ravens were able to travel between this plane and the void. Their energy added great value to his ceremony and would be the key to lifting her past the final barrier to enter the Spirit World. His gratitude for the corvids' help could not be expressed because it was so expansive. There were simply no words for the magnificence of Great Spirit and the creation of the All.

Katrina was nearly convulsive when he started his song to the keepers of the West. Simultaneously aware of her and of the power growing around them, he remained focused on his part of the ceremony and ignored the return of the bats. At first, the flapping of wings in his peripheral vision told him more ravens were coming to his call, but the rapid beating of bat wings was so opposite from the graceful swoop of the ravens' that his attention became mildly diverted.

He knew if he stopped drumming and singing he would have to start over from the beginning. Based on Katrina's persistence to fight him every inch of the way, he did not want to forestall this any further.

The bats moved in closer to him and the cage of twigs around Katrina. All at once, he noticed the increase of gnats and insects tickling his face. They landed on his lips while he sang the song. They zoomed into his nostrils and bit the corners of his eyelids. Bats chased the bugs in every direction and he was once again surrounded by paper-thin wings and tiny clawed feet. Blinking furiously, he refused to let Katrina's bats stall him. The gnats were being ground between his molars and coating his tongue, but he kept singing.

When he finished the call to the West, he placed the drum on the ground and turned to check on Juliana. Her eyes were closed against the swarm of flying insects and she waved both hands around her head in an attempt to ward off the attack of bugs and bats, but she held her ground.

When Chris turned around, he saw Katrina's diversion working. The bats were inadvertently breaking up his shield keeping Katrina above ground. She'd also managed to work her mouth free of the red clay powder and screamed at him.

"Where is Billy? I knew you were lying to me! He loves someone else and not me. You're both liars! Where's Patty?"

Her body pressed against the remaining twigs and feathers. Bats darted and flapped around the cyclone, breaking it up little by little.

"Jules, keep your mouth and eyes closed!" he yelled. If anything went wrong in the next minute or two, he didn't want her body and spirit compromised. Great Spirit knew she'd already experienced enough spiritual trauma this year.

Juliana didn't reply and he didn't have any more precious seconds to waste on her safety. He had to react now or Katrina would be lost again. He dove for his prepared satchel. When he rose, Katrina was right in front of his face. A large bat flew between them and he instinctively pulled back to protect his eyes from the wings. Chris must have gasped because an insect flew down his throat. It was a rookie mistake to breathe in with a malicious ghost hovering inches in front of his face, but he'd done it.

He coughed up the bug and watched an evil and bitter smile spread from cheek to cheek on Katrina's young face. She saw her opportunity and entered Chris's mouth, taking up residence in his airways and effectively blocking all air from entering or leaving his lungs.

Cursing himself for allowing her a way to enter his body, Chris remained as calm as possible and put aside all distractions—Juliana's panicked whimpers—apparently her eyes were open now even though he told her to close them—and the feeling of suffocation from Katrina inhabiting his mouth, nose, and throat.

His fingers worked at the satchel with steady competence. Now that Katrina was distracted by attempting to kill him, her control of the bats and their persistence on catching the swarm of flying insects lessened. This helped exponentially in allowing Chris to remove his tools from the leather bag.

The feeling of the smooth round stone in the bottom of the bag was an immediate relief. He popped it into his mouth and pressed the polished rock to the roof of his mouth, holding it in place with his tongue.

The minerals in the stone combined with the power he'd infused into the rock chased Katrina out of his system like a firestorm. Chris anticipated her next move and he reacted with super reflexes.

Katrina's spirit dove for the crevice in the rocks, and her favorite hiding place deep inside the mine. Juliana's mouth was clamped shut but her eyes were wide open. As fate would have it, his apprentice saw the ghost coming at her and raised the raven foot talisman into Katrina's face. It stalled the girl just enough to allow Chris the second he needed to cast the raven feathers at her.

He spit the stone from his mouth back into the bag and commanded, "With wings of the sacred raven, go from this Earth and travel unburdened to your waiting ancestors!"

The ravens in the trees came down from all directions. A flurry of iridescent-black bodies and all-knowing eyes surrounded Katrina. Juliana flung herself to the ground and out of the way as the whoosh of air from the powerful wings fought for control and maneuverability around one spirit girl. Chris held a circle of protection around the immediate area and felt a deluge of both relief and anxiety engulf him.

He watched, listened and prayed as the ravens stripped Katrina of her fears and madness. Her imbalance would not pass into the next world. Chris could feel her psychosis shedding and it wasn't a pleasant feeling. Juliana was most likely experiencing it as well, but he knew in the long run it was good for her to get another experience under her belt.

"Embrace the peace of your true self. Travel with a clear heart, Katrina."

"Billy," she sobbed one last time.

"Move now! Go to your soul's dwelling place. Great Spirit embrace this girl!"

He raised his satchel overhead and shook it at the sky. The ravens rose above him, lifting with them the cleansed spirit of Katrina Caldwell.

* * *

"Magpies? Really?"

"You do not have to sound so doubtful, Jules. The magpie is an intelligent bird and a cousin to the raven."

"What did the feathers do to her?"

Chris turned right onto the paved road that would lead them back to town. Juliana surprisingly didn't require any recovery time after Katrina's passing. She was definitely shaken but appeared in decent control of herself. He'd done a simple cleansing and prayer ritual for his spirit and for Juliana's and she'd held her tongue. Chris also needed minimum first aid applied to the scratches on his face and arms. Juliana helped him and seemed genuinely worried about the risk of infection. After washing his skin with bottled water, she dabbed on some antiseptic ointment from a first aid kit she carried in her backpack. Then they had hiked to his pickup truck in silence. Both of them needed time to integrate all that had happened with Katrina. Now that they had a few miles between them and the location of Katrina's departure, Juliana's torrent of questions had begun.

"The magpie moves on his own terms. He has an unusual way of approaching new situations. Magpies are good birds."

"And..." Juliana prompted.

"I used the power of the magpie to build a nest of sorts to capture Katrina from her chosen home. Then I let the bats carry her outside. It was a hunch that it would be a successful tactic. Bats are powerful creatures of transformation. I knew they would seek the sky when the sun lowered. I could not release her spirit within the confines of the mine. Too much stone and not enough sky. The raven was sent to me for this case and I had to get Katrina to more of them." Chris gave a nod of finality to close the subject.

He watched her bite her lip and take a breath. Juliana turned slightly in her seat and watched the road. To his surprise, she held the rest of her questions. No matter how annoyed he became with her at times, she was making out to be an excellent apprentice. Grateful for the quiet, he took advantage of the long drive to work through his own need for mental processing of Katrina's case as they headed to the Mancos residence.

Chapter Six

"I WANT YOU to pay attention, but leave the talking to me," Chris said.

She crinkled up her face with mild discontent. "Whatever you say, Chief."

"Juliana, we were getting along so well. Don't ruin it," he said with more contempt than he'd meant.

The long day and the fact that neither of them had eaten since morning wasn't helping the tense situation. They had both agreed that even though food would help their crabby attitudes, neither of them had any sort of appetite. The stress and terror at the mine and now having to confront Billy and Patricia Mancos left them both uneasy.

"I'll buy us dinner after we take care of the dirty details of this case," he added as a way to help smooth over what he'd just said. Chris knew he could be too brash. The attitude of distrust and dislike for other human beings had been his way since birth. Sometimes he made attempts at getting along with people, but mostly he avoided other humans knowing it really was him. Regardless of his faults, he appreciated Juliana's help today and he needed to at least pretend to show it.

And, in truth he valued Juliana's thoughts and opinions, but in this case he only wanted her to observe. If she did what he asked, she would soon see why she should remain quiet for this part of the job.

She tapped her shut lips and raised haughty brows at him as if to say her mouth was already sealed tight.

He knocked on the green front door and waited.

Billy answered and stood aside so they could enter. Patricia laid cold eyes on them, lingering particularly on Jules in an unwelcoming way.

"Let's move to the dining room," Billy said.

Chris explained that he had found Katrina and helped her cross over to the Spirit World. He didn't give the details of how he practiced his sacred medicines, but assured Billy and Patricia that Katrina was now at peace.

"Can you fathom it, Billy? All these years..." Patricia reached over and placed her hand on her husband's arm.

"Garrett is going to be beyond himself. Do you think his bad dreams will stop now?"

"I believe so. If he dreams of her now, it will only be in remembrance, not a visitation," Chris said.

Many shadows crossed over their faces as Chris told them what he wanted them to know. Billy's face and aura was a fair bit easier to read than his wife's, but Chris was learning more and more about this couple by the minute.

"Did you actually speak with her?" Patricia asked.

Her concern didn't range much farther than to only serve her selfish purposes. Chris knew this truth like he knew his shoe size. She worried for herself and her part in her cousin's disappearance.

"Not much," he said vaguely.

Juliana sat to his left and he heard her clear her throat.

"I communicate with the Spirit World in multiple ways. You should focus on her safe return to Creator. That is all that matters, Mrs. Mancos."

"But did she tell you what happened after Billy left her inside the mine?" the woman insisted.

Billy's fingernails turned white on the tips as he pressed his hands against the wood surface. Chris kept his gaze steady and his face blank.

"She did not. It was interesting finding your cousin at all. You neglected to tell me she disappeared inside the old mine. I went east first and could not pinpoint her location." He paused and waited for Patricia to speak.

Her eyes darted right and then left, refusing to make direct contact with Chris. "I'm sure I told you she was inside the mine. That's where all four of us were that day."

"No. You did not say. It hardly matters now if you left out that part of the story. I found her. I did use alternative methods to remove her from the mine before performing the ceremony, but be assured it was successful."

"Was she…umm…did she look okay?" Billy asked awkwardly.

"Just as you described her," Chris said.

"I never meant for anything bad to happen. I just want you to know that. It was all a huge misunderstanding."

The man's face reddened as he tried to say something about Katrina or the past. It wasn't coming out well. Patricia put a stop to her husband's verbal fumbling.

"It was a horrible tragedy. We're so grateful for your help, Mr. Abeyta. I need to call my brother immediately and tell him what you've shared with us." She rose from her seat and urged Billy to rise as well.

Her plastic tone was almost too much for Chris to take. He'd like nothing better than to out her and her husband and tell them he knew everything. Even if Katrina's version of events was slightly askew, he knew in the pit of his soul that the couple had been cruel to the girl because they were hiding their feelings for each other from her. And at the time, apparently from Garrett as well.

"You two were a couple and she didn't know it," Juliana said accusingly.

Chris gave her a flat look that warned her to be quiet.

Juliana shot him a look back that said she wouldn't keep quiet. He sighed.

"Why didn't you just tell her?" Jules asked.

Patricia turned to face Jules. Billy sat motionless in his seat.

"Garrett didn't know about our feelings toward one another and we didn't want him to know yet. He was going off to college and I wasn't. We thought if we could just wait a few more weeks, then he'd be gone and we could date openly and we'd tell him later."

"They don't need to know all this, Bill," Patricia said, placing her hand on his shoulder.

"But what happened after you left her inside the mine?" Juliana asked.

Chris knew Juliana's flood of questions had risen and was now spilling over. Patricia didn't want to talk about it anymore, but Billy looked like he needed to.

"I was angry. Patty and I went back to the Wagoneer. Garrett was past being pissed, but he wouldn't leave Katrina alone. He went back to get her and I was going to go with him but Patricia wouldn't let me. She was furious about Katrina groping me. I shouldn't have told her at all but I was afraid Katrina would make up other more detrimental lies. Garrett showed up hours later and said he couldn't find her."

"That's enough. None of it matters now. Katrina had an accident and that's that. I'll tell Garrett what you told us. Thank you, Mr. Abeyta."

Juliana turned her green eyes on Chris. Her energy field harbored a mixture of emotions and a fair amount of anger.

"You're all guilty, you know that. You left her in there because you were angry that she kissed your boyfriend. You abandoned your cousin," she said to Patricia. Then to Billy, "And you kissed her and made her cry. In Katrina's messed up way, she loved you. Yes, she had an accident, but all of it could have been prevented if you'd just told her the truth to begin with."

"That's enough, Juliana," Chris said, rising from the chair.

"But—"

Patricia looked horrified by Juliana's outburst. Billy looked like he wanted to be forgiven.

Chris didn't want to speak another word to these people, but managed to say, "We'll see ourselves out. Thank you for your business."

* * *

"Lying is ugly," Juliana said as they drove away from the house. "Mrs. Mancos didn't even want you to find her and Billy... Gah! He's missing a pair, isn't he? I could feel their guilt and regrets like cold slime."

"What happened to remaining quiet?"

She stuck her tongue out at him. "Those people suck."

"All three of them, Billy, Patricia, and her brother Garrett, played a part in her disappearance, but it was Katrina's stubbornness and her own error in judgment that killed her."

Juliana crossed her arms over her chest. "I guess," she said with a pout.

"That is how I would explain it. Garrett perhaps was the innocent party in all this. I believe that is why she found him in the dream land."

"Are you going to the police?"

"I have a friend who works for the department. I will make a report. Her body won't be recovered based on where you thought it was located and chances are there will be very little left to find."

"Bleh," Juliana said from her side of the truck and shook all over like a dog ridding itself of water.

"Sounds about right," Chris said agreeing with her distaste for human remains.

"Maybe they can recover the gold locket. I wonder if her parents are still alive."

"I don't know. What I do know is, people like closure. I have to call Garrett Sanchez and update him. I'm sure he'll contact anyone who needs to know. He is the stable one in this trio. If my officer friend needs to talk to you, I will pass along your number."

"Stellar," Juliana said. "I think every cop in the county knows me by now anyway, so what's one more interrogation?"

"It will not be an interrogation. You did nothing wrong."

"You're right, I didn't. Besides, Billy and Patricia's lies, or should I say, omissions of the truth should be exposed."

"Lies often start out for one reason or another. Sometimes they can be justified. The Mancoses protected themselves. They had their reasons. After a long time the lies become truths. It is sad and dangerous. Even the story Katrina told you may be mixed with little white lies."

Juliana let out a long heavy breath. "Is everyone unstable in some way?"

"Possibly. The best you can do is to not forget it."

"Great. We're all crazy. Just great."

Chris let out a small snort. She wasn't totally wrong in her assessment.

Juliana stared out the passenger side window. "It's strange that the four of them have all existed with different versions of the same story. I don't like it. The lies were twisted up with the truth and it makes it hard to discern what really happened."

"I did not like this case from the moment my phone buzzed. It showed me that even though I can tell when someone is being deceitful, it doesn't mean they are in the wrong. There are times when doing what is right means putting your own feelings aside and doing it anyway."

"Yeah, but it's hard."

"True. Katrina needed our assistance. That is what matters in this case."

"I know, but, man...she kind of tried to kill you."

"I've had easier cases," he admitted.

"And what exactly was I supposed to learn from all this anyway?"

He didn't answer. Instead he pulled into the parking lot of a diner. "Before we open that can of worms, we need to eat."

* * *

After a quick bite to eat, they were back inside the pickup truck and heading toward home. Juliana had indulged herself on soup, salad and coconut cream pie. Chris had the open-faced turkey sandwich. Food had been the cure they both needed after the long, taxing day.

"Spirits can get stuck. Think of them as lost in their own minds even after the body has perished," Chris said as they cruised down the highway. "It is not dissimilar to people who continue to repeat an unhealthy behavior over and over again. The loop a spirit can be in is often much shorter or simpler and often very disturbing."

"Katrina was stuck on Billy. When she died she could only think about the situation that happened right before her death. Is that correct?"

"Yes. I think she had a mild mental or emotional imbalance before she died inside the mine. When she had the accident it magnified her problem."

"That's really sad." Juliana squinted her eyes as if it might help clear her inner vision. She took a deep breath and let it rush out of her in a long stream. "Did you seriously bring me with you to learn about ghost's mental problems?"

"Take away from this experience the parts that speak to you. Lessons are often learned in a way that is separate from the intentions given by the mentor."

"I'm not willing to accept that answer. What did you really intend for me to learn?"

"Experience, Juliana. That is your lesson. Now it's up to you to learn something or not. You always seem to have a thousand questions. Since I am stuck with you inside this cab for the next hour, now would be the time to ask what you want to know."

"*You* are willing to answer *my* questions?" Her look of skepticism could have been a caricature.

"It is a onetime offer, so do not get used it, Ant. Your help was needed and I am willing to pay you with my time. Remember, wisdom is always in the question."

"Hmmm…" she said, making a thoughtful noise. "Okay, when did you start wearing vests as everyday attire?"

His silent pause and look of hopelessness for the future of mankind made Jules laugh.

"What?" she asked wearing joyful innocence on her youthful face. "You said I could ask you anything I wanted."

Absurdity and impatience oozed out of Chris. Juliana's impish smile widened.

"I don't know when I started wearing them. Maybe in college," he said through clenched teeth.

"Are you going to kidnap me again for your next ghost hunting trip?" she asked more seriously.

"Are these the kind of questions you ask when seeking to find wisdom?"

"Hey, I'm just asking what comes to mind in the moment," she said innocently.

"Then I highly doubt you'll be accompanying me on my next case."

She stuck her tongue out at him—again. It seemed to be a recurring theme for the evening. He shook his head with annoyance but grinned back at her.

About the Author

Jody A. Kessler is a USA Today bestselling author. Her debut novel, *Death Lies Between Us*, book one in the *An Angel Falls* series, is the winner of the Readers' Crown Award for Best Paranormal Romance. She writes contemporary romance, historical time travel fiction, and paranormal fiction. She is the author of the An Angel Falls series, Granite Lake Romance series, The Night Medicine and more.

When Jody isn't navigating the terrain of her imagination and writing it down, she can be found exploring the wilderness of Colorado with her family, or in the kitchen baking cookies & brownies – and trying not to eat them all. She's passionate about continuing to learn and reads anything and everything that catches her interest.

Jody A. Kessler invites you to stop by her website and see what's new at: www.JodyAKessler.com. You can also connect with her on Facebook at Jody A. Kessler, or on Twitter @JodyAKessler.

For updates on future releases you can sign up for the newsletter on Ms. Kessler's website.

From the Author

I would like to say a special thank you to John, Nancy, Jamie, Simon, my family, friends, beta readers, and fans for their continued support. I couldn't do this without you.

Made in the USA
Middletown, DE
31 January 2023

23586110R00104